The slap reve[...]
like a pistol s[...]

Before the interrogator had a chance to utter another word, Bolan entered the fray, lunging through the doorway in a crunch. Four hardmen stood around a fifth, who was seated in a wooden chair.

It took three parabellum rounds to sweep the head man off his feet. Dismissing him, Bolan tracked on the others, who were scrambling for their hardware. Left to right, the Executioner stitched a line of bloody tracks across two gunners, leaving only the fourth, who jammed a snubby .38 in the captive's ear.

"Your call," the Chinese gunner snapped. "You wanna rock and roll with me, you gotta dance with this guy first. Or maybe I just blow his head off for the fun of it."

"Suits me," Bolan replied, shrugging.

"You're bluffing, man."

"Keep thinking that. It makes my job easier. Fact is, I came to kill you bastards. I care squat about this guy. Want to take him out? Go ahead."

"Just who the hell are you?"

"Does it matter?"

Then the Executioner made his move....

MACK BOLAN.

The Executioner

DON PENDLETON'S
THE EXECUTIONER.
FEATURING MACK BOLAN.

HAWAIIAN HEAT

A GOLD EAGLE BOOK FROM
WORLDWIDE.

TORONTO • NEW YORK • LONDON • PARIS
AMSTERDAM • STOCKHOLM • HAMBURG
ATHENS • MILAN • TOKYO • SYDNEY

First edition November 1991

ISBN 0-373-61155-2

Special thanks and acknowledgment to
Mike Newton for his contribution to this work.

HAWAIIAN HEAT

The wise man in the storm prays God not for safety from danger, but for deliverance from fear.
> —Ralph Waldo Emerson

It is fatal to enter any war without the will to win it.
> —General Douglas MacArthur

I have my target, and I've offered up my prayers. The will to win was always there. This time I'm fighting on the beaches to destroy a beachhead, rather than secure one. History will have to say which side came out on top.
> —Mack Bolan

To America's frontline soldiers
in the war against illegal drugs.
God keep.

Mack Bolan had been following his targets for almost half an hour, waiting for the perfect opportunity to strike. It hadn't been a problem in the urban sprawl of downtown Honolulu, with the lights and traffic to distract his prey, but it became a different game once they were on the open highway, rolling east beyond the signs for Diamond Head and following the coastline. Here, away from the diversions of the city, one mistake could be the hunter's last.

The full moon helped, allowing him to run without his lights when there was no competing traffic on the road, resorting to the low beams only when another vehicle appeared. With any luck, the changes would relieve suspicion in the lead car, reassuring his selected targets that they weren't being followed after all.

Assuming that they cared.

The snatch had been a textbook exercise in arrogance, performed with blatant disregard for witnesses. The team had done this kind of work before, and the men knew that they were good. If anyone attempted to prevent them from accomplishing their goal, the opposition would be dealt with.

Harshly.

Outside of Honolulu, east of Diamond Head, Highway 1 became Highway 72, scaled down with the decreasing flow of traffic, rolling through the darkened countryside with ocean on the right, then Koolau Mountains hulking like a prostrate dragon on the left. Past Koko Head and north, the highway wound along a coastline that was sometimes pristine sand and sometimes rugged cliffs of stone. Bolan had the landscape memorized, but he wasn't a tourist. Focused on the lead car's taillights and his rear-view mirror, watching out for new additions to the game, his full attention had been concentrated on the hunt.

One option would have been to interrupt the snatch it-self, but he had weighed the odds and found them skewed in favor of the opposition, threatening a bloodbath if he tried to burn the gunners on Kalakaua Avenue. Too many passersby, for starters, and the urban battleground would give his targets too damned many holes that they could hide in, using the advantage of familiar ground to shake him off the track. And, in the meantime, you could bet your life that they would waste their mark, for spite if nothing else.

All things considered, it was better if he gave them room to run.

Their destination would depend upon the players. Two of them at least had been Chinese. That narrowed down the options, but the game was still complex enough to keep him guessing. There was no room for assumptions at the present stage, when everything he had was riding on the line.

Or, more precisely, riding in the car ahead.

He lost the taillights short of Makapuu, devoured by a narrow side road, but the moonlight kept him more or less on track. Another moment, and the lead car's driver kicked his headlights onto high beams, compensating for the sudden loss of pavement, palms and other vegetation edging close on either side.

Bolan took his time and let his quarry blaze the trail. He wouldn't risk his headlights on the side road, even with the lead car out of sight. There might be sentries waiting for him up ahead, and while he couldn't spare the time required to ditch the car and make his way on foot, at least a dark approach would give him some advantage of surprise.

Assuming, always, that the lookouts weren't equipped with Starlite scopes or infrared equipment that would pick him out as clearly as a cockroach on a butcher's block. If they were zeroed in with night scopes . . .

No, the men he sought were pros, but they were hardly soldiers. Pickups on the street and contract killings fell within their realm of expertise, along with rough interrogations and the art of staging lethal "accidents;" but every instinct told him they weren't prepared for total war.

It was their crucial weakness, and the Executioner's major strength.

A soldier all his life, he was prepared to fight the war at hand with any means or tools at his disposal. They didn't know who they were playing with, proceeding out of blissful ignorance that someone new had joined the deadly game.

It was the kind of clumsy oversight that got men killed.

He glimpsed the house from a quarter mile out, lights burning in the second-story windows, overlooking darkened grounds. He made another hundred yards before he parked the car, its dome light disconnected, showing nothing as he cut the engine off and opened up the driver's door to stretch his legs.

The house was good news. It reaffirmed the snatch team's need to keep their mark alive, however briefly, while they tapped his brain for information. They would count on some initial reticence and pull out all the stops if necessary, but they wouldn't kill until their questions were exhausted, answered to the satisfaction of the man who paid the bills.

If he could tag that man tonight, it would be so much simpler, but the warrior knew enough to concentrate on first things first.

And first things, here and now, included preparations for the probe.

Beneath the roomy slacks and jacket, the blacksuit, fitting like a second skin, would provide him with a cloak of near invisibility while granting him the freedom he required to make each movement count. He wore a custom-tailored shoulder rig, with the selective-fire Beretta 93-R slung beneath his left arm, two spare magazines in pouches underneath the right. A military harness, buckled to the pistol belt around his waist supported ammunition pouches and grenades, a Ka-bar fighting knife, the heavy Desert Eagle automatic riding on his hip.

Without a head count on the enemy or some assessment of their arms, he was compelled to pack another weapon, compromising weight and firepower in the interests of combat mobility. The standard Uzi submachine gun fit his needs precisely, with its folding stock and cyclic rate of fire that could reduce a man to steak tartare in seconds flat. The chunky silencer would slow things down a trifle, but it wouldn't matter much at 750 rounds per minute off the mark.

He locked the car and primed its dual defensive mechanisms. Any hostile touch would trigger an alarm approximately loud enough to wake the dead, continuing until the battery ran down or the device was properly deactivated with a special key. If the alarm wasn't enough, and more determined efforts were employed to breach the vehicle, a string of C-4 plastic-explosive charges were in place to help the prowler on his way.

The moon was partially obscured by a drifting veil of clouds as the warrior struck off across the road and disappeared inside a field of cane, a tracker's instinct leading him in the precise direction of the house. It was slow going in the field compared to travel on the open roadway, but he stood a greater chance of meeting lookouts with the obvious approach. This way, if there were snipers in the cane, he stood at least an even chance of spotting them before they cut him down.

The darkness and the tropic undergrowth were like a second home, familiar from the days and nights in Southeast Asia and a hundred other jungle killing grounds. Hawaii was a piece of cake: no lethal snakes or spiders, nothing in the way of enervating heat that sapped a soldier's strength and will to fight.

The enemy had taken no great pains to light the grounds around their safehouse, finding security in the remote location and the snatch team's talent to ensure they weren't tailed. Approaching from the west completely unopposed, Bolan gave them points for nerve, then subtracted from their score for suicidal arrogance.

It showed when gunners became overconfident. You saw it on their faces sometimes, after they were stretched out in the morgue.

He came around a corner from the unprotected front and found the solitary lookout zipping up his pants, a dazed expression on his face, as if the act of urination somehow had evacuated brain and bladder simultaneously. He was dead before he had a chance to reach the shotgun propped against the stucco wall, the muffled flutter of a 3-round burst inaudible beyond the nearest windowpane.

So far, so good.

One down, and if they didn't have an army packed inside the smallish house, he might have shaved the odds by ten percent or so. It made a decent start, but any one of them could drop him if he let himself relax.

The back door wasn't open, but a moment with the Kabar cleared the way. He stood inside a kitchen redolent with fish and soy sauce, smells that conjured images of Oriental street bazaars. The fantasy was reinforced by muted voices arguing in Cantonese, one room away.

He didn't speak the language, but the hunter understood the tone. His marks were on the verge of a falling-out, perhaps in a debate about the proper means of handling their prisoner. Technique was everything in an interrogation, but there were a thousand different ways to get results, and each had its defenders when the chips were down.

A new voice interrupted, cutting through the cross talk like a heated blade through cheese. The others might have been disgruntled, but they kept their complaints to themselves. From the sound of things beyond the flimsy door, the inquisition was prepared to move ahead.

At last the hunter heard a voice he recognized. No matter that it had been years—a lifetime—since they'd spoken.

"I guess I pissed you fellas off, is that the story? Listen, if you took offense to the routine, I offer my sincere apologies. It's like we got a failure to communicate or something. Did you ever see that movie by the way? Terrific actors, there. But I was saying—"

"Silence!"

The commander's voice. A man in charge, accustomed to obedience.

"You don't want I should talk, all right. Hey, who am I to argue with the host?"

The slap reverberated like a pistol shot. Bolan winced, his finger tightening around the Uzi's trigger as he took a long stride closer to the door. It would have been a treat to turn the tables, choose a hostage of his own for questioning, but something in his gut was saying that the play would zero out to all or nothing. Once across the threshold, he'd have to do or die, and "doing" meant that no one else came out alive.

Except the smartass, right.

Before the lead interrogator had a chance to speak again, the Executioner joined them, lunging through the kitchen doorway in a crouch and leading with the silenced Uzi. Four men were standing, three behind and one before a fifth man, who was seated in a wooden chair.

In doubtful situations, the leader should be taken first, on general principle. Confusion was the first result, and if a warrior played his cards right, that initial edge might be the only break he needed.

It took five parabellum rounds to sweep the head man off his feet, a dazed expression on his face that caught him somewhere between a curse and scream. Dismissing him from all consideration while the corpse was airborne, Bolan tracked on the gunners who were still alive and scrambling for their hardware.

Left to right, the warrior stitched a line of bloody tracks across a pair of living bookends, firing inches over the scalp of one he meant to save. The impact punched them over backward, out of frame, and that left only number four—the quickest of the lot, as he discovered, glancing to his right and wincing as his adversary jammed the muzzle of a snubby .38 inside his captive's ear.

"Your call," the Chinese gunner snapped. "You wanna rock and roll with me, you gotta dance with this guy first. Or maybe I just blow his head off for the fun of it."

"Suits me," Bolan replied.

"You're bluffing, man."

"Keep thinking that. It makes my job easier. Fact is, I came to kill you bastards. I don't care squat about this guy. Want to take him out? Go on. If you don't I'll have to zip him open for a chance to waste your ass."

"And who are you supposed to be?"

"Does it matter?"

"I think you should lay that fucking Uzi down before I count to three, or Smartass here can start to rent his skull out as an ashtray."

"Like I told you—"

"One."

Bolan watched his adversary's eyes, deciding that he meant it. There was no bluff in the Asian's stony gaze.

"And two."

"Okay, you got me."

As Bolan reached out to drop the Uzi with his left hand, his right slipped back at speed to free the Desert Eagle from its quick-draw holster as he fell. He aimed between the straight legs of the chair, between the captive's feet, and fired a quick round at the Chinese gunner's knee.

He triggered another round and his man went over, sprawling on his back, the snubby .38 forgotten in his fist.

Suddenly stillness settled over the house of death, and Bolan scrambled to his feet in front of the captive tethered in his chair.

"You took your own sweet time," the man said. "Those goons were just about to play a game of Chinese Ping-Pong with my face."

"Relax," Bolan answered, finally loose enough to smile. "With that skull of yours, their paddles never would have lasted through the serve."

2

"This feels like Old Home Week, you know?"

The wise guy's name was Tommy Anders, famous as a stand-up comic on the Vegas and Atlantic City circuit, less well-known for his involvement with the U.S. Justice Department's Sensitive Operations Group, in charge of busting Mob connections to the entertainment business and beyond. His passing reference hearkened back to other times he'd worked with Bolan, other times when a strategic intervention by the Executioner had saved the comic's life.

"At your age," the soldier chided, "I was hoping that you'd have found yourself a less exhausting line of work."

"We're counting birthdays now? Don't tell me you've been talking to my agent."

"Does he know about your sideline?"

"He's a she, my sexist friend—and no, she doesn't. Bad enough she has to settle for a second billing when I press her on a special job. I don't think she could take it if she knew why I was *really* so particular about the spots I play."

"Hard times?"

"Times change," the comic answered with a shrug. "Right now it's in to go four-letter all the way, or stand up there and scream like you've got crabs the size of pit bulls. Subtle's definitely in the shade these days."

"Hang in," the warrior said. "This, too, shall pass."

"You're telling me? I've seen more fads blow through the trade than I can shake a dick at. Next street on your right."

They turned off Rycroft Street, just short of Piikoi, moving into upscale residential as Anders made a point of scanning sidewalks and the cars parked close on either side.

"Two down and on your left."

An older building, fashionable in its way, but still a cut below his usual accommodations. Bolan drove on past, eyes tracking, circling once around the block before he let the comic guide him to a private parking area in back.

"Don't say it," Anders warned as they left the car. "It's better inside than it looks, and nothing in this neighborhood comes cheap. Besides, it's clean."

"Is that confirmed?"

"It better be. I booked it through a cutout with our good friend Leo."

Smiling at the reference to a trusted mutual acquaintance on the Justice desk in Washington, Mack Bolan still took time to slip the single button on his jacket, granting quicker access to the sleek Beretta worn beneath his arm.

In case.

They rode the elevator up to number four. Bolan let himself relax a bit when they were safely locked inside the apartment, Anders fussing over a coffee maker in the kitchenette.

"No wires?" the warrior asked.

"I checked it out this morning. If you want to play it safe, I've got an FM unit in the bedroom."

"Right."

Before he left the living room, the Executioner took time to turn on the television. Oprah was smiling at a blonde whom Bolan knew he should have recognized, congratulating her on completion of her latest movie. Nothing real, but it would do.

He fetched the FM radio and took it with him to the center of the living room. It was a fact that most surveillance bugs transmitted over open FM bands not allocated to an active station in the bugger's given theater of operations. With simplicity in mind, the system made it possible for listeners to park outside—or cozy up in an apartment blocks away—and listen to their mark by tuning in a common radio, without procuring any kind of specialized receivers. It was easy and effective, but the method also had its weaknesses.

With Oprah and her guest for background noise, the Executioner turned on his radio and started scanning through the numbers, moving slowly up and down the dial. Transmitters weren't selective in their output, meaning that an FM bug in Tommy's flat would beam its message out to *any* set that happened to be tuned correctly. If he found a number on the dial where Oprah and the busty blonde came back to him in stereo, it meant the place was wired.

"Okay," he said, when he'd run the circuit twice. "We're clean, as far as I can tell. Let's talk."

"Hal sent you?" Anders asked, setting the coffee on a narrow breakfast counter, one man sitting down on either side.

"He said the islands might be warm this time of year. Your name was mentioned, with some Eastern players. Not exactly what you'd call an overdose on the specifics."

"Left that to me, I guess. Okay. For openers, we're talking major narco traffic from the East. Some retail, sure, but basically Hawaii is a perfect staging point for shipments to the mainland. Mostly heroin right now."

"What else is new?"

"The players. Five, six years ago it was a family operation down the line, with blessings from the capos in Los Angeles and San Francisco. New York and Chicago had their fingers in the pie. Today, if you speak Italian in the trade no one understands a word you say. There's been an east wind blowing through the islands, and it isn't blowing anybody any good."

"The Yakuza?"

"For starters. Japanese make up a quarter of the population in Hawaii, and you don't need me to tell you most of them are honest to a fault. The trouble is, they've got an estimated hundred thousand scumbags back in Old Nippon, all pushing drugs and women, running down protection rackets on the side, and now the gangs are spreading out just like the honest businessmen. They don't advertise their presence, but they're out there."

Bolan knew what Anders meant. In recent years, the Yakuza—Japan's native Mafia—had surfaced in Los Angeles, San Francisco, Las Vegas, New York and a score of other cities coast to coast. Legitimate investments ranged from sushi bars and posh hotels to gambling casinos and dog tracks in states where betting was legalized. Observers from Justice had no doubt the Yakuza trailblazers were still involved in more traditional pursuits—narcotics, white slavery, extortion and international gunrunning. Bolan had crossed paths with the Japanese Mob more than once, and he recalled them as grim, do-or-die opponents, clinging to a twisted image of the ancient samurai code.

"You're giving me a history lesson, Tommy."

"Make it current events. The Yakuza has put down solid roots in Honolulu, with one Kenji Taoka calling shots for the Ichiwa-kai faction. Up front, he's Mr. Philanthropy, big in construction and charitable donations. Japan's gift to the West, if you get the drift."

"Sounds familiar."

"Okay. On the flip side, he's dirty as hell, but we can't make a case that will stick. He's got buffers on buffers, this guy. Seven murders we're sure of, this year, but nobody talks. I mean *nobody*. Honolulu P.D. picked up one of his shooters last spring and caught him with an unregistered piece. Definite no-no, and potential trouble for the family if it was ever traced back to a source."

"Fat chance."

"You got the picture. Anyway, our little bird in jail lost face and had to make a gesture of repentance to his *kuro-maku*—that's the Yakuza equivalent of a 'godfather.' First, he tried to hang himself, and when he couldn't pull it off, they caught him trying for a deep six in the toilet bowl. Again, no dice. The jailers put him under suicide watch, stripped his cell—the usual. Two nights later the guy made it. Chewed through his own wrists—both of them, mind you—and bled himself out before breakfast."

Sipping at his coffee, Bolan felt a chill, remembering fanatics he'd known. They couldn't always be identified by race or creed, but sometimes, if you leaned in close enough to check their eyes, you caught a hint of something missing. Rationality, perhaps, or simple fear. Fanatics didn't give a damn what happened to themselves or anybody else, as long as they accomplished their appointed missions, "saving face" along the way.

"Somebody's fingered this Taoka for a hit," he said.

"Somebody, right, but not in Washington. The story's got a flip side, guy."

"I'm listening."

"You saw my friends tonight."

"They were Chinese," Bolan put in, helping Anders reach his point.

"Affirmative. Thus enters ball club number two."

"The Triads?"

"Chu Lien Pang, to be precise. You drop that name in Hong Kong or Macao, and you can clear a room real fast—or find yourself a prime connection for the purest China white."

"A drug war?"

"That's the reading. Free market competition, with a twist. Oahu's shaping up to be the new Miami. You've got drive-by shootings, disappearances and drug burns, DEA involvement, right on down the line. If money's not enough, throw in the racial animosity between Japan and China, dating back to who knows when, and you've got all the makings of a major shitstorm."

"Who's coaching for the Triads?"

"Ho Yuan Lee, a heavy hitter out of Bangkok. He's got solid-gold connections with suppliers in the Triangle, and his reputation speaks for itself. An estimated thirty—that's three-oh—assassinations of competitors in Thailand, with a handful here since he arrived."

"Still nothing in the way of witnesses?"

"The Chinese don't believe in telling tales."

"What kind of action are we looking at?"

"So far, a fairly standard territorial dispute. The families were edged out over time by federal prosecution and the native competition. Nothing they could do about it, once the boys from Justice started pulling down convictions. There was no one left with weight enough to save the game."

"Tough luck."

"For some. The Yakuza delegation was tickled pink, until it started facing competition from the Triads. They've always managed to coexist, as long as things were on a minor scale, but nobody likes to share a bonanza. Justice is convinced we're looking at a mini-World War III, unless somebody caps the well.''

''And we're elected?''

''More or less. I've spent the past two weeks examining some options, feeling out the territory. Neither side is unopposed within their own community, but getting anyone to testify is something else. Nine out of ten may hate the Triads and the Yakuza, but they're still scared to death. Both sides can bend your ear about their friends and relatives who tried to buck the Mob on some protection scheme or signed complaints against a dealer. If you've seen one funeral, you've seen them all.''

It was an old, familiar story to the Executioner. An honest, decent people terrorized by outlaws in their midst, afraid to risk their lives and families to break the chains.

''I'm not concerned with logging testimony,'' he reminded Anders.

''No, but there's another angle. I've made certain contacts that we might find useful. People that the syndicates have pushed around.''

''Civilians?'' Bolan shook his head. ''It doesn't work that way. I'm not recruiting for a citizens' militia, Tommy. Pass your contacts on to Justice.''

''They won't talk to anyone official, but they don't mind getting in a lick against their enemies if they can pull it off without a lot of state and federal paperwork. So far they've given me a list of targets, contacts, things you could find useful if you take the job.''

''I've taken it already,'' Bolan said. ''But don't expect a slow dance by the numbers.''

''Hey, I've seen you work, remember? Honolulu's ready for a shake-up. Hell, it's overdue. Sometimes I think the town was better off when Frankie Olivera ran the show.''

''And King Fire?''

"Well . . ."

"It's no good looking back," the Executioner declared. "We play the cards we're dealt and bet the limit when we can. If you think I need to meet with your civilians, set it up, but first I want to test the waters on my own. You mentioned names?"

"All kinds, both sides. I won't pretend to finger every hostile body on the island, but I've got a fair start on a *Who's Who* for the heavies."

"Fair enough. I need a place to start."

"You want the bottom or the top?"

"I'll take a sampling of each. No point in telegraphing my intentions, if I've got a choice."

The comic poured another round of coffee, settling on his stool. "Feels like old times," he commented.

"Let's hope it feels that way tomorrow, or the next day."

"Right. You plan on rattling some cages?"

Bolan's smile was weary.

"Is there any other way?"

3

Closing on the first target of his new Hawaiian campaign, Bolan reflected briefly on the history of his diverse enemies. He knew, for starters, that the Yakuza dated from the early years of the seventeenth century, when rural bandits and rogue samurai first joined forces to prey on the wealthy ruling class of Japan, cutting themselves a slice of the solid-gold pie. Over time, loose-knit societies of gamblers, thieves and assassins were organized into clans or "families" in the traditional Mafia pattern, nurturing a code of silence and "honor" that any born Sicilian would have recognized on sight, despite the language barrier. Fiercely nationalistic and ultra-conservative, Yakuza leaders helped push Japan toward a disastrous military adventure in the 1920s and 1930s, climaxing in the nuclear fire storm that consumed Hiroshima and Nagasaki. Ironically, the syndicate had risen from those glowing ashes more or less intact, the anti-Communist persuasion of its leaders making them natural choices for leadership positions under the occupation regime of General Douglas MacArthur. Yakuza money and muscle were used to crush fledgling radical movements—and organized labor unions—in the late 1940s and early 1950s, strengthening the Mob's already substantial economic and political ties as a new Japan emerged to dominate world trade in automobiles and electronics.

By the 1960s, Yakuza watchers from Tokyo to Washington, D.C. reported the existence of nine distinct syndicates, including some 2,300 affiliated criminal gangs and roughly 100,000 members overall. From strongholds in Japan, their network spanned the globe, including solid footholds in America. Japanese mobsters had arrogantly dubbed Hawaii the "forty-eighth prefecture," staking their claim to local traffic in drugs and women, while the state's Yakuza Documentation Center compiled active dossiers on some 7,000 syndicate members known to operate in the islands. Each year 800,000 tourists from Japan passed through Hawaii, and their numbers offered members of the outlaw class an opportunity to lose themselves amid the crowd.

In the late 1970s, when various Yakuza factions began muscling in on the American heroin trade, undermining the death grip of traditional Mafia families, Hawaii served as a natural staging point for shipments of poison in transit from Southeast Asia to the mainland. Stateside distribution was disguised behind the operation of investments that included country clubs, hotels, casinos, restaurants and health spas, but the Japanese incursion on a long-established empire hadn't been devoid of strife.

For openers, the Mafia wasn't prepared to see the golden goose fly east without some effort to retain control, and Justice had recorded several bloody clashes on the narcotrade frontiers. The Executioner himself had been a witness—and behind-the-scenes participant—when soldiers of the Yakuza invaded the Sicilian turf around Las Vegas, and his intervention had resulted in a draw, of sorts, with neither faction coming out ahead. Elsewhere, the Mafia had lately seen its ranks depleted by attrition—gang wars, state and federal prosecution, sheer old age—and competition from the Yakuza was coupled with substantial inroads made by Cubans and Colombians, Iranians, Vietnamese . . . and members of the Chinese Triads.

Once again, the warrior plucked a mental file and scanned the stats from memory. According to tradition, the Triad syndicates—or Tongs—were almost as ancient as the Yakuza, founded as a self-defense society by Buddhist monks around Foochow, in Fukien province during 1674. From simple self-defense, the early Triads drifted into revolutionary politics, taking another leaf from Mafia history as they schemed against the oppressive Manchu regime. Their cause would ultimately prove to be a losing one, but from political defeat emerged a different sort of triumph, the creation of a network that would span the Chinese empire, taking root and infiltrating every walk of life. The Tongs were firmly rooted in America before Congress passed the Chinese Exclusion Act of 1882, and by the turn of the century, wily "celestials" dominated the stateside opium traffic, turning additional profits from illegal gambling and white slavery. Hatchet men affiliated with the rival On Leong and Hip Sing Tongs fought bloody wars from coast to coast a generation prior to Prohibition, and it took new federal laws to drive their power underground.

At home, The Triads boosted revolutionary Sun Yat-sen in his ascent to power, and Sun's successor—Chiang Kai-shek—was an acknowledged member of the society, relying on mercenary thugs to fill the leadership ranks of his Kuomintang regime. Mao's victory in 1949 spelled doom for the Triad societies, resulting in summary execution or imprisonment for thousands of recognized gangsters, but thousands more escaped to Hong Kong, Taiwan, Singapore, and Southeast Asia's "Golden Triangle," where their cultivation of opium continued with minimal interruption from Maoist opponents. As with the postwar Yakuza, the anti-Communism of the Triads endeared them to short-sighted Western diplomats, and three decades of conflict in Indochina established enduring links between Triad leaders and fringe elements of the American intelligence community.

Full-scale infiltration of North American was inevitable under the circumstances. Relaxation of immigration standards opened the floodgates for 300,000 Hong Kong immigrants between 1965 and 1980, plus countless thousands of illegal aliens. By the early 1970s, thriving Triad colonies, were recognized in Vancouver and Toronto, San Francisco and New York City, Los Angeles, Boston and Chicago. The traditional On Leong and Hip Sing rivals were present in substantial numbers, but authorities recognized a total of nine competing Triad societies, numerically matching the Yakuza with an estimated 100,000 members worldwide. Their contacts in the Golden Triangle gave Triad spokesmen a decided edge in moving China white—the purest and most potent heroin available—and Chinese brokers found they could name their price in dealings with the Mafia. In time, as the Sicilians fell away, the Tongsmen went into business for themselves. Once more, Hawaii was a valued staging area—and a potential battleground—as the competing Triads sought to move their lethal product through a territory dominated by the Japanese.

Despite their five-percent minority in the Hawaiian islands, Bolan knew that the Chinese—and, more specifically, the outlaws in their midst—weren't prepared to stand aside and be ignored or trodden underfoot. The enmity between Chinese and Japanese predated World War II.

Statistically Mack Bolan knew his enemies shared common strengths and weaknesses. The Chu Lien Pang society was China's fourth-largest Triad, based on Taiwan, with an estimated ten to fifteen thousand members scattered over Southeast Asia and North America, with footholds in the Middle East. By contrast the Ichiwa-kai was Japan's fifth-largest Yakuza faction, a relative newcomer to the underworld scene, organized in the early 1980s. Smaller than the rival Triad, with an estimated 3,000 members, Ichiwa-kai could rely upon 140 affiliated gangs for reinforcements in wartime.

And when it came to killing, Bolan knew, the Japanese would never be intimidated by sheer numbers of their opposition. The Triad's founding fathers might be credited with the invention of kung fu, but history had turned a page since territorial disputes were fought with swords and open hands. The military equalizers currently available to anyone with ready cash to spend ensured substantial body counts whenever ruthless rivals came to blows.

And it was looking like Old Home Week on the islands, all right. As Bolan lined up his approach to target number one, his thoughts were drawn inevitably back to a previous Hawaiian conflict, played out in his early one-man war against the Mafia. It had been Frankie Olivera's territory then, with Tommy Anders pitching for the Justice team. Bolan had unearthed a link between the syndicate and pointmen for the Chinese Communists. The code name for their grim cooperation had been King Fire, and the Executioner had added several fiery touches of his own. The end result had been a flameout for the savages, with Bolan's side emerging more or less intact.

Each new campaign of Bolan's everlasting war was different in its way, but at the bottom line, his enemies remained the same. Their faces and political affiliations changed from time to time, and they communicated threats in different tongues, but all of them were savages at heart. They preyed upon the weak and helpless, wreaking havoc in society as they pursued their goals without regard to law or personal morality. Experience had taught the Executioner that only one response would serve when cannibals assembled for the feast.

He was about to teach the savages a lesson in reality, beginning with his own version of cause and effect.

When the savages encountered Mack Bolan, an explosion was inevitable.

Hawaii was edging toward critical mass.

4

It was after midnight when the soldier turned his dark sedan off Palolo Avenue, cruising into the neighborhood known as Saint Louis Heights. He kept the sprawling state university campus on his left, using the dormitories as a landmark on unfamiliar ground, searching out the first address he'd obtained from Tommy Anders.

Bolan's target was a whorehouse. Nothing flashy, but the kind of place a lonely tourist with a bankroll could relax and spend an hour—or an evening—with a sympathetic partner, sampling the wonders of a world that he, or she, would never find at home in Cincinnati or Saint Paul. According to reports, some locals patronized the house as well, but everything was geared toward tourism in the Aloha State, and this discreet class act was no exception. The establishment catered to every taste, and the management made certain no one went away unsatisfied.

The operation thrived by word of mouth, but one small detail generally omitted from the advertising spiel was its connection with the Yakuza.

The patrons couldn't speak of something that they didn't know, and while the cash kept flowing in, the secret owners were content to stay anonymous.

Mack Bolan hadn't asked about the comic's source. It didn't matter in the short run, and he had a feeling that he'd be meeting Anders's contacts soon enough, despite his own desire to leave civilians out of what was coming.

He made the address—a colonial design, three stories, soft light showing through a window here and there—and circled the block to find himself a parking place. The only angle of approach that he could count on was a john in search of happy times.

He'd have to improvise. It was a skill that he'd honed to near perfection over time, in killing situations where his instinct was the first line of defense.

He parked against the curb, avoiding any risk of being bottled up inside the driveway. When the play went down, he'd be operating strictly by the numbers, and the plan didn't include a late arrival's Cadillac or sports car cutting off his only exit.

On edge, his combat nerves alert, the short walk up the driveway seemed to take forever, Bolan conscious of the night around him and the weight of the Beretta underneath his arm. The small incendiary sticks distributed in various pockets wouldn't show unless they used a "sniffer" to detect the chemical ingredients, and he was confident that no such tight security would be in place.

He rang the bell and waited thirty seconds before a butler dressed in formal evening wear appeared. The guy was native, tall and muscular. He scanned the new arrival with a glance comprised of two parts curiosity and one part thinly veiled suspicion.

"Yes, sir?"

"I lost my invitation, I'm afraid, but Mona is expecting me."

"This way, sir, if you please."

In fact, there was no "Mona," but the name served nicely as a password, changed at monthly intervals unless specific circumstances called for a revision in security procedures. Bolan was relieved to find that Anders had been given current information by his contacts.

The decorators of the house had tossed conservatism out the window, dressing up the place with velvet curtains, textured paper on the walls, elaborate chandeliers and hand-carved furniture. A hint of incense in the air could not disguise the smell of marijuana emanating from a private party room upstairs.

The butler led his charge into a sunken living room, where half a dozen beauties lounged on easy chairs and sofas, wearing wispy bits of nothing. Every color of the human rainbow was on hand, a smorgasbord of sex, with practiced, plastic smiles. Bolan picked out two more working ladies at the wet bar on his right, giggling their way through a conversation with the Japanese bartender. The barkeep—like the butler—wore a dinner jacket with a not-so-subtle bulge beneath one arm, denoting hardware in an armpit sling.

"Your pleasure, sir."

The butler left him as an "older" woman—all of thirty-five, he guessed—appeared from somewhere on his left to take delivery of the new arrival. In another setting, Bolan guessed her low-cut gown would pass for daring, with its flashy show of cleavage, but compared to all the other goodies on display around him, she appeared reserved and businesslike.

"You must be Mona."

"Close enough. And you are . . ."

"Passing through," he told her. "What I need right now is for your girls and paying customers to step outside."

The smile began to falter. "Step outside?"

"Unless they like their meat well-done."

The woman dropped the smile. "Is this some kind of joke? I don't know what the hell—"

He let her see the Beretta, silencing her question as he thumbed the hammer back and swiveled toward the bar, his first round shattering a hundred-dollar whiskey bottle on the bottom shelf.

The barkeep saw it coming and he made his choice. Instead of throwing up his hands or taking to his heels, he made the grab for hardware, cold eyes narrowing to slits as he perceived the hopeless odds.

It was a sucker bet, and Bolan shot him once, the parabellum round impacting squarely on his forehead, exiting in back to spatter crimson on an ornate mirror behind the bar. The shooter melted out of sight, a fading memory, before the startled working girls began to scream.

Their chorus brought the butler back at double time, a shiny automatic in his fist. A quick one-two at point-blank range dissolved the sprint into an awkward, tumbling sprawl, and Bolan had a sidelong glimpse of Mona fading back before the dead man's body came to rest.

He caught her by the arm.

"How many more?"

"I don't—"

"If you've got muscle in the house I want to see it. Now!"

"One man. Upstairs."

Around them, seminaked girls were scrambling for the nearest exit. Bolan let them go, his full attention focused on the stairs and the ceiling smoke alarms.

"If you've got any special way of clearing out the rooms you'd better use it. Thirty seconds."

Seeing that he meant it, Mona turned and marched directly to the wet bar. Bolan covered her and hoped she had more brains than courage as she leaned across to key a hidden switch. At once, the upper floors reverberated with a mellow sound of chimes, reminding Bolan of an Asian temple bell.

It did the trick. Doors sprang open, footsteps rushing toward the central stairs and several exits Bolan couldn't see from his position in the living room. No matter. He was interested in clearing house, and it would make no difference if the occupants decamped through hidden doors or up the chimney, just as long as they were out before the place went up in flames.

To his relief the madam circled back around the bar and came out empty-handed, showing no desire to join the hired help on a one-way trip to the morgue.

"What else?" she asked.

"That's all. Go home."

"This *is* my home."

"I hope you've got insurance, Mona."

"Bastard."

"Mona?" Bolan's voice reached out and caught her at the door. "Tell Kenji this is just a start."

He'd already scattered half a dozen of the small incendiary sticks, a couple of them sputtering to angry life before the final gunner showed himself. A cautious man, he'd been waiting to decide the nature of the threat, aware that it would be a critical mistake to open fire on uniforms. The first alarming whiff of smoke made up his mind, and Bolan heard him coming, heard him rack a live one in the riot shotgun's chamber as he moved along the upstairs hall.

At thirty feet the scattergun's reliability was flexible, depending on the size of shot employed. A buckshot round would give the gunner an advantage—simply point and squeeze—while solid slugs would mean he had to aim his weapon like a rifle. The smaller shot would be no good at all. Eliminating risk, the Executioner was waiting when his target lumbered into view, the 93-R set for 3-round bursts and steadied in a firm, two-handed grip.

One squeeze, and Bolan saw the big man stagger, lurching back against the nearest wall. Another, and the ornate pattern of the paper on the wall acquired new texture, sprouting viscous lumps before the lifeless straw man slithered to a crouch.

He waited long enough to see the flames take hold and start to feed, the smoke alarms announcing danger to an empty house. A portion of the structure might be saved, if they were wired directly to the nearest firehouse, but he doubted that the Yakuza would take that step. Instead they'd prefer to salvage what they could, disposing of incriminating evidence before the trucks arrived with squad cars in their wake.

Too bad.

Taoka was about to take a loss on his investment, and it didn't matter if the house was covered by the best insurance in the world. Most policies excluded acts of war, and Bolan's personal campaign for the Hawaiian hellgrounds had begun.

THE CHINATOWN CASINO wasn't large by mainland standards, but it made the most of floor space, packing customers around the gaming tables and along the bar where watered drinks were sold for twice the normal going rate. While fan-tan was among the dominant attractions, visitors could also try their hand—and lose their cash—at craps, roulette and blackjack.

Once again, his contact had supplied a name that opened doors, and Bolan spent a moment on the smoky threshold of the gambling den, absorbing sights and sounds before he made his move. He took a moment to locate the two opposing exits, each secured by a pair of

Triad hardmen, and he drifted counterclockwise, following the wall until the entrance lay ten paces to his left.

It was a different layout than the whorehouse, with a different clientele, and Bolan had decided on a different gambit going in. Step one would be attracting the attention of a crowd enraptured by the sight of money on the table, the excitement of potential fortunes riding on the wheel, the cards, the dice. No easy task, but Bolan had a ploy in mind.

He slipped a hand inside his jacket, well around in back, to find the smoke grenade secured to his belt. The doorman hadn't noticed the bulge when he scrutinized the new arrival, checking Bolan from the front, and the casino's various security precautions didn't include a metal detector at the entrance. Caught up in their games, no one appeared to notice the warrior as he palmed the military canister and yanked the safety pin, tossing it overhand toward the middle of the crowded room.

It landed in the middle of the roulette table, jolting chips and currency away from numbers covered by the bettors. In a flash, before the players could react or recognize the object, dense white smoke erupted from the canister, competing with the smell of cigarettes and strong cigars. No contest in the bustling room, and panic followed seconds later when a cocktail waitress started screaming "Fire!"

The warrior followed her instructions, leveling the mighty Desert Eagle, squeezing off two rounds that sounded like a single clap of thunder, instantly submerged by shouts and screams. Across the room a pair of sentries were reacting to the smoke grenade when Bolan's double punch blew both of them away, the hollowpoint projectiles ripping flesh and bone asunder with explosive force.

The smoke-and-gunfire combination touched off a stampede, with gamblers, waitresses and dealers surging toward the exits, elbowing the slower refugees aside. Directly opposite Bolan, thirty feet away, the two surviving hardmen had their guns in hand, attempting to determine what was happening.

It was a tricky shot, with bobbing heads and hairdos in the way, but Bolan put his faith in years of battlefield experience, the Desert Eagle braced in both hands as he sighted down the slide and stroked the heavy weapon's trigger one more time. The echo of his shot produced a shock effect, like ripples in a pond, with bodies lurching away from his position, jostling together as the multi-hued, amorphous organism of the crowd tried desperately to save itself.

His bullet found its mark and punched the taller of his targets back against the door, where he was swiftly overwhelmed and trampled underfoot by the mob rushing toward the street. The dead man's partner saw his danger, ducking underneath the line of fire and disappearing momentarily.

If he was smart—if he could move—the shooter would be angling for a new position, working on an angle to return the killing fire. His first reaction, dodging out of sight instead of spraying bullets aimlessly around the room, let Bolan breathe a trifle easier. The crowd would work against them both until it started thinning out and they were gradually exposed.

And Bolan didn't intend to wait around that long.

He spied the manager, a tux in motion, bulling through the crowd, and moved to head him off. Bolan threw an arm around the guy's throat from behind and dragged him aside, allowing other bodies to pass them in a mad rush for the door. He applied pressure, waiting for the slender man to give up struggling and stand at ease.

"I've got a word for Ho Yuan Lee," the warrior snarled. "You copy?"

Rapid nodding gouged the other's chin against his biceps.

"Tell him that the heat's just starting. Any questions?"

The manager's head twisted in a desperate negative.

"Unless he likes the smell of smoke, your boss should find himself another place to play."

Before the man could nod his understanding, Bolan caught a flash of movement on his right, a single body struggling upstream against the human tide.

It was the gunner, trying for an easy kill.

The Executioner swung in that direction, dragging the manager in front of him as two rounds cracked across the open space between them. One snapped by on the left, a miss, but number two drilled through the manager's tuxedo, scoring flesh along his side.

The Desert Eagle answered with a blast that left ears ringing. No time to aim, but Bolan's instinct made it work, the hollowpoint on target as it ripped through flesh and fabric, driving his opponent to the floor.

The manager was squirming in his grasp, and Bolan recognized the musty scent of urine as the guy lost all control. He might be too far gone to quote the soldier's message word for word, but he wouldn't forget their confrontation, and the gist of Bolan's threat would come across.

For now it was enough.

He let the walking wounded go and caught the tag end of the fleeing crowd, becoming part of the determined exodus. The streets were in chaos, residents and straggling tourists pressing forward to catch a glimpse of smoke and rumored fire, the recent gamblers and a handful of employees taking to their heels before police arrived.

The Executioner refused to hurry. He was parked four blocks away, and he knew that running figures drew more attention to themselves. He was content to let the normal flow of traffic carry him along and out of Chinatown.

Two down, but he wasn't prepared to let it go just yet. His warnings had been tendered and would duly be received, but any lesson worth the learning called for reinforcements, a dramatic demonstration to complete the process of assimilation in the brain.

His enemies were men of cunning, weaned on treachery, the fine points of the double cross. Before he finished with their education, both the Yakuza and Triads would be forced to cope with the reality of grim defeat.

The Executioner was blitzing on.

THE LUXURIOUS apartment building stood on Olohana Street, its upper windows offering a long view of the Ala Wai Canal. The doorman moved to intercept Mack Bolan as he entered, but the warrior flashed a gold, all-purpose badge and breezed past in the direction of the elevators. Knowing the apartment number in advance, he didn't have to ask and thereby tip the watchdog to his destination. There'd be no hasty phone calls to announce him or alert the enemy.

His target didn't occupy the penthouse, though he might have made it, given time. As second in command of Honolulu's Yakuza, Sachiro Matsumoto was a wealthy man, accustomed to respect from those beneath him. Pushing forty, he was old enough to know the ropes and young enough to yearn for some excitement, once removed. In time, if everything went well, he might command a family of his own.

But time was short, and things were going sour for the Yakuza in Honolulu. Starting now.

Impending warfare notwithstanding, it would never do for sentries to be posted in the hallways of a ritzy Waikiki apartment building. Assuming there were guards—and Bolan knew it was a fairly safe assumption—they would be inside the suite with Matsumoto, fulfilling their duties to the *kuromaku*'s number one.

If the warrior tried to pick the lock, the slightest sound would give him away, and there was still the possibility— make that the probability—of extra bolts and chains inside. The sleepiest of sentries would have time to draw a bead and blow him away before he got inside.

Likewise, the blitz approach. It was within his means to kick or blast the lock, but either way meant noise, and the delay occasioned by a hidden chain or dead bolt could be fatal.

That left option number three, a blitz with frosting on it, and he had the silencer-equipped Beretta in his hand before he knocked on Matsumoto's door.

It took a moment for the gunners to decide on a response. He pictured them examining their watches, frowning as the hour registered. The boss might be asleep, and they'd have to think about consulting him before they answered. Was it wise to roust him out of bed before they knew the caller's name and business? How would Matsumoto take it if they woke him to confront some boozy visitor who had mistaken the apartment number or the floor?

He was prepared to knock again, and keep on knocking, when a muffled voice responded from beyond the door.

"Who is it?"

"Blake. Security."

The name and tag were meaningless, but implications of an urgent message just might do the trick.

"What do you want?"

He muttered something incoherent, lowering his voice to make sure the nonsense syllables got lost.

"What's that again?"

He mumbled again, softer this time. A latch was thrown, the doorknob turned, and he was looking past the chain into a single eye. Its owner didn't seem amused.

"Security, you said?"

This time he let the 93-R do his talking for him, the message loud and clear despite the silence. One round between the door and jamb, directly through that staring eye, and Bolan threw his weight against the flimsy chain, its anchor ripping free and dropping to the floor.

Inside he found a second gunner waiting, dumbstruck by the leaking body at his feet. Before the guy could reach his automatic, another parabellum closed the gap between them, canceling all opposition.

The Executioner closed the door behind him, hoping that the only noise so far—the snapping chain—hadn't been loud enough to wake the neighbors. Stepping over the prostrate forms, he scanned the combination living room and kitchen for a backup team, found nothing as he navigated toward the master bedroom.

Darkness cloaked the far side of the threshold, and he entered in a combat crouch, his free hand groping for the light switch, finding it before his target could respond to the vibrations of an unfamiliar presence in the room. Sachiro Matsumoto sat up, blinking at the light, satin sheets bunched around his waist.

A glance took Bolan back to childhood carnivals, when he and brother Johnny prowled the midway, checking out the freak show and the illustrated man. Sachiro Matsumoto was a work of art, his upper body decorated by designs of dragons, serpents, tigers, floral sprays—a second skin of many colors, covering his chest and torso, darkening his arms from shoulders to a point not far below the elbow.

And if any proof was needed of the guy's connection with the Yakuza, the Executioner was looking at it. Not for nothing were the native mafiosi of Japan described as "tattooed men."

"Who are you?"

If the disappearance of his bodyguards concerned him, Matsumoto did a decent job of covering the fact.

"Keep both hands out where I can see them," Bolan cautioned, moving closer to the bed.

"I asked—"

"I heard you. Let's just say I've got a message for Taoka."

The tattooed gangster risked a smile and glanced around the bedroom. "As you see, he isn't here."

"You'll do. It's your choice whether you relay the word or I take time to write a note and pin it on your body."

Matsumoto lost his mocking smile at that.

"I'm listening."

"I hope so. Kenji's hunger is about to spark a shooting war. In fact, I think you'll find the first shots have been fired already. By the time you read your morning paper— if you live that long—you'll have a fair idea of what I mean."

"This war . . . does it concern my family?"

"It should, since you're about to lose it."

"Really?"

"Bet your life. You didn't think that Master Lee would just sit back and let you steal his territory, did you? Maybe you've been reading fairy tales."

"May I assume you work for Lee?"

"I don't much care what you assume. The fact is, you're not dealing with some penny-ante operation in the sticks. Lee has connections stateside, friends who wouldn't want to see their flow of product interrupted."

"Ah. You represent these friends."

"I follow orders. If someone says 'Take care of Matsumoto,' I don't ask them why. I do the job."

"*Are* those your orders?"

"You're still breathing, aren't you?"

"What, then?"

"A message, like I said. Some people figure China white should come from China, if you get my drift. They don't buy sushi when they've got a taste for egg rolls."

"But if I could make your friends a better price—"

"Not my department. You want marketing. I handle overdue accounts."

"Of course." The guy was cool, Bolan had to give him that. "I'll relay your message to my sponsor. In return perhaps you could communicate with yours."

"We chat, from time to time."

"A chance to deal. Negotiation is the heart of any business. Wise men recognize the need for mutual accommodation."

"That's the spiel?"

"Of course we would expect to compensate your friends for any inconvenience that a change in dealerships might cause."

"I'll pass it on, but I won't promise anything. If they send me back to see you, chances are there's nothing left to say."

"My men?"

"You're going to need some more."

"No matter. They were paid to take the risk."

"That sounds familiar." Bolan kept the tattooed gangster covered as he edged back toward the door. "I hope they're paying you enough."

He half expected Matsumoto to attempt some move, but there was nothing as he crossed the bedroom threshold, moving out of there before the Yakuza lieutenant could retrieve a weapon and pursue. Outside, he caught the elevator, rode it six floors down and disembarked, descending service stairs to reach the street.

Again, he had anticipated a reception in the lobby, but the doorman made a point of concentrating on a magazine as Bolan passed. Upstairs, Sachiro Matsumoto would be on the telephone by now, but odds were long against him calling the police.

Taoka's housemen would be answering the call in no time, and a cleanup crew would be dispatched to take care of the stiffs in the suite. From there, the Yakuza reaction would be anybody's guess.

It stood to reason that the Japanese had made connections with a major network in the States, and Bolan had refrained from dropping any names or geographical associations, just in case. Regardless of Taoka's standing deal, it also stood to reason that the Triads had connections of their own. An Asian shooting war in Honolulu could have mainland repercussions, and it wasn't stretching credibility to let Taoka think some branch of the established Mob was gearing up to back the Chu Lien Pang defense.

And if an Anglo gunman was connected with the recent strikes against both sides...

The Honolulu game was warming up.

It wouldn't be much longer before the men on top began to feel the heat.

5

The *Tokyo Rose* was an eighty-foot beauty, all white with a hint of blue trim that was mirrored in some of the fittings, upholstery and gear. She slept twenty in comfort, her galley producing a mess that was classic gourmet. On a cruise, guests could fish or shoot skeet from the fantail, get high on a dazzling selection of liquor and drugs, or adjourn to their staterooms with their pick of the females who made up two-thirds of the crew.

In short, the yacht was a classic executive party boat, and her ownership papers traced back to a Yakuza front on Kauai. Job one for her commander and his crew had been seduction of assorted politicians and executives in business, law-enforcement officers, attorneys—anyone, in short, whose goodwill and assistance might advance the syndicate's designs in the Aloha State.

When not at sea, the *Tokyo Rose* was berthed at Ala Wai Yacht Harbor, an easy five-minute stroll from Waikiki Beach. On his approach, Bolan knew no parties had been scheduled for the next three days, and members of the crew wouldn't be lingering on board at dawn, in any case. A guard or two, perhaps but he'd cross that bridge when he came to it.

He turned the dark sedan off Ala Moana Boulevard, winding his way toward the water, and found a parking space with little problem as the first gray light of morning tinged the skyline to the east. From where he sat, the yacht was visible beyond a line of smaller vessels, windows dark against the eerie glimmer of the bulkhead.

Bolan heard the numbers running as he stood beside the car, stripping off his slacks and jacket to reveal the midnight skinsuit underneath. It took him several seconds more to fetch his rigging from the trunk and buckle it in place, abandoning the Uzi and its extra magazines in favor of an OD satchel weighing close to twenty pounds.

A little something special for the *Tokyo Rose*.

He took no pains to cover his approach until the yacht was clearly in view, aware that guards wouldn't be posted over the marina as a whole. No lights were showing, but the sentries wouldn't make a point of advertising their locations. Not if they were any good, at least.

And if they weren't, it made his job just that much simpler.

With twenty yards of open dock before he reached the gangway, Bolan hesitated, studying the ship from stem to stern. It took a moment, but he caught a hint of movement on the foredeck—possibly a silhouette of head and shoulders hunched against the starboard rail—and if they had one man on duty topside, there should be another below deck.

He took a chance and crossed the open ground with long, swift strides, the silence-equipped Beretta in his hand.

The sentry missed him on the gangway, and the oversight was all the edge that Bolan needed. Circling around the cabin, he took the foredeck sentry from behind, before the guy had time to realize that death had come to claim him.

One more glance verified the target, just in case Taoka's captain might have stuck a cabin boy with graveyard duty. The hardman had his jacket off, and Bolan made the pistol in his shoulder rig as one of Smith & Wesson's automatics, chambered for the same 9 mm parabellum round that his Beretta used.

The gun was all he had to see.

A hard rap on the temple with the butt of the Beretta put the sentry into dreamland, long enough for the warrior to make his play.

One down. How many left to go?

The classic set would place two men on board, but Bolan had survived this long by tossing all assumptions out the window. He had the time to spare—not much, but it would do—before he kept the next appointment on his list, and he couldn't afford to be surprised while he was on the yacht.

A door stood open aft, below the flying bridge, and Bolan slipped below deck like a shadow, gliding down the companionway. The smell of cigarette smoke drew him forward past the galley until he reached a combination lounge and game room. Muted lights hadn't been visible from topside, and it followed that any troops below were unaware of Bolan's presence on the ship. He spent a moment on the threshold, studying the set before he made his move.

Two gunners lounged in overstuffed chairs on opposite sides of the room. Both looked bored, one smoking listlessly, the other thumbing through a magazine with all the interest he might have shown while waiting in a doctor's office. Killing time, no doubt, before the next man drew his shift on deck.

At a slight sound both gunners looked up, reaching for their hardware when they spotted their uninvited guest. Bolan shot the smoker first, one round through the forehead, and the gunner died with an expression of surprise on his face.

The reader dropped his magazine and tried to save himself with a reaction that was almost quick enough. Almost. He reached his gun before the first 9 mm round smacked home, the impact rocking him against the cushions of his seat, but he'd never have a chance to draw and fire.

The C-4 plastique was divided into two-pound packets, as soft and pliable as putty in his hands. He planted them strategically below deck, starting with the engines and the fuel tanks, taking time to wire the galley, leaving blocks to serve the bulkhead, fore and aft, below the waterline. Each charge was fitted with a detonator, timed to blow at quarter-second intervals, with number one on tap six minutes down the road.

The timing was precise and left no room for error, but it gave the warrior ample opportunity to put some space between himself and the ship.

He was nearly back to the sedan when number one went off like clockwork, shattering the engines, touching off a secondary blast as fuel tanks joined the conflagration. After that, the chain reaction was a stunner, shattering the early-morning calm and raining shrapnel over the marina, oily clouds of smoke and flame obscuring the dawn.

As thunder rolled across the harbor, Bolan finished stowing his equipment in the trunk, deactivated the sedan's security device and slid behind the wheel.

He still had work to do before he got in touch with Tommy Anders for another meeting. Bolan's targets weren't expecting him, but the surprise was everything. It was his edge, and he needed every ounce of leverage he could get.

The Executioner didn't believe in playing favorites, and it was time to share. The Chu Lien Pang society was scheduled for a party its local members would recall as long as they survived.

For some of them, another hour ought to do the trick.

WHEREVER TOURISTS GATHER in substantial numbers, women, drugs and liquor are available in quantity, regardless of prevailing law. Demand dictates supply, and if one broker fails to meet the public's need, he'll inevitably be supplanted by more capable competitors. Hawaii— frequently depicted in publicity releases as an Eden free from violent crime and drug abuse—is no exception to the rule.

The Executioner had done his homework, and he knew that Hawaii's annual rate of property crimes—burglary, larceny, auto theft—and overall offenses equaled or surpassed the standard U.S. averages. While rape and murder lagged behind, both categories had been catching up in recent years, and overworked police were looking at a grim new day of violence in the streets. As everywhere across the country, many of the recent thefts, assaults and slayings were directly traceable to drug abuse, a growing problem that Hawaii shared with mainland states.

In the narcotics trade, Hawaii had become a thriving market *and* a relay station for illegal shipments moving westward, bound for Canada and the remaining United States. On the side, production of Hawaiian marijuana— famous on the mainland as Maui Wowie, Puna Purple or Kona Gold—was a major industry, generating some $600 million per year and financing various well-organized, well-armed gangs to handle distribution in the islands. Most of the street-level gangs were native Hawaiian—an ethnic stew comprised in equal parts of Polynesians, haoles and Asians—but Eastern leadership had started to assert itself in recent years, providing new connections and allowing local operators to expand beyond their wildest dreams.

One such was Benny Kapioliani, small-time hustler, gunman and extortionist turned millionaire on profits from illicit weed. To give the devil proper credit, Benny had conceived the shift in occupations on his own, and he'd financed early stages of the move. But when it came to cracking mainland markets, he was forced to take on partners with sophistication and experience.

The Triads, for example.

Ho Yuan Lee had recognized a young man with initiative, and he'd offered only small suggestions as he took the job of empire building firmly in his hands. If marijuana was a major seller, Benny could increase his profits twentyfold by putting heroin and other potent potions on the menu. Lee had contacts in the East and on the mainland, sources and distributors whose goods and expertise were readily available. The service was a bargain, when you thought about it—eighty percent of first-year profits shifting to Lee and company in return for a few phone calls—and doubly so when Benny thought about the various alternatives.

Like death.

Or worse.

In any case, twenty percent of millions was better than one hundred percent of thousands, anyday. Despite his status as a grade school dropout, Benny knew math well enough to add up dollar signs.

And dead men earned no money whatsoever.

So, the warehouse off Nimitz Highway, fronting Honolulu Harbor, had been rented out of Benny's end. Why not? It was a minor price to pay for affluence, and when you thought about the monthly rent as life insurance, it began to make more sense than ever.

Fifteen hundred to his landlord on the first of every month, and Benny bought himself a little peace of mind.

Or rented it. Whatever.

Bolan knew about the warehouse and its contents from his chat with Tommy Anders at the safehouse. Twenty minutes into daylight, he was circling the block and checking for security devices at a distance, wondering if Benny would be paranoid enough to station snipers on the roof. No sign of lookouts, but a slipup could be fatal once he showed himself.

He parked downrange and walked back to the warehouse, carrying a satchel similar to one that he'd left aboard the yacht. Before he reached the loading dock, he knew that there wasn't a sentry on the roof, perhaps no one inside. A lookout worth his paycheck should have noticed an approaching stranger, carrying an OD parcel at that hour of the morning, and he'd have offered some response.

That didn't mean the place was empty, necessarily, but it encouraged Bolan, all the same. If Benny had a man inside, the guy was sleeping at his post.

He got the simple lock first try, the tumblers falling into place as Bolan probed them gently. As he expected, there was no alarm. In case of robbery the tenants wouldn't want detectives prowling through their stock, discovering their cache of outlaw pharmaceuticals.

Across the threshold Bolan scanned the warehouse, checking out a glassed-in office to his right, the rows of wooden crates and cardboard boxes stacked in front of him, divided up by aisles that would accommodate a forklift. No sentries inside.

The satchel held ten thermite canisters, and Bolan used them all before he left the warehouse, starting at the far end, pitching left and right across the crates and cartons. Before he reached the exit, most of the grenades had detonated, spewing clouds of smoke and white-hot coals that ate their way through wood and cardboard, steel and concrete.

Bolan had no way of knowing where the drugs were hidden among the countless crates, so he took the only course available and torched it all. If any of the products stored therein were scheduled for delivery to legitimate concerns, the stock would be insured. As for the lethal contraband...

If Bolan listened closely, he imagined he could hear Lee screaming even now. A warm-up to the main event.

It was full daylight as he left the place behind, smoke curling through the melted skylights and the open door.

It didn't matter what the fire department did from that point on. The thermite would consume itself in time, and anyone who tried to interfere without a fair supply of specialized equipment would be spitting in the wind.

IT WAS A MOST UNGODLY hour for a phone call. David Chan was wide awake before the second ring, although he never answered calls himself. It was the houseman's job to screen incoming messages, disposing of the trivia and passing on the calls that mattered.

Chan shifted on his pillow, studying the bedside clock, and grimaced. Only bad news came that early in the day. He waited, sitting up and ready when the houseman knocked.

"What is it?"

Trouble showed on the gofer's face, as if he couldn't quite decide on a response.

"Guy wouldn't give his name," the houseman said at last. "He told me someone burned the warehouse, and you'd better take his call unless you want the fire to spread."

"No name?"

The houseman shook his head and shrugged, a curiously awkward combination of responses. "Like I said, boss. But he has your private number, and he knew who he was asking for."

"Apparently. All right, I'll take it. Curtains?"

Chan sat motionless until the man pulled the heavy draperies wide open, early sunlight slanting through the bedroom windows, catching motes of dust suspended in midair. He reached for the receiver only when he was alone.

"Hello?"

"Good morning, David."

"Do we know each other?"

"I know you. I know your boss."

"If I could have your name..."

"I'll give you something better. All the news that's fit to print. Your people have a warehouse at the harbor?"

Chan had been around too long for anyone to dupe him with a simple question on an open line.

"My various associates lease many properties. If you would care to be specific..."

"Benny K. You want a name, try that one on for size. A fire just cleaned him out. Are we communicating now?"

"If you have information on a fire, perhaps you ought to speak with the authorities."

"You, first. In case your people start to think it might have been an accident, I want to clear that up. You play with fire, sometimes you get your fingers burned—or worse."

Chan forced a smile, delayed his own response until he felt the anger fading. "I was never any good at riddles, Mr...."

"Names again? Okay, try Matthew. You're familiar with the Matthews, I believe."

Chan stiffened, recognizing one of several inside nicknames for the Mafia.

"Perhaps if we could try one subject at a time, we might make progress."

"That's exactly what we're doing, David. All one subject. You, and Mr. Lee and Benny K. All lining up against the Matthews, cutting in on territory that's been spoken for. I knew you were supposed to be inscrutable, but dumb is something else."

"I don't respond to threats or insults, Mr. Matthews."

"Fair enough. Let's try a message from on high."

The line went dead ... or, rather, it was open, humming with a sound of distance, but the caller had apparently abandoned his receiver for a moment. It was curious, somehow disturbing.

David Chan was trembling as he said, "Hello?"

And then he bolted out of bed, as something struck the bedroom window, showering the room with bits of broken glass. Eight floors above the street, and he was scurrying for cover, stunned that anyone could find a way to penetrate his home.

Behind him on the bed, a gunshot echoed from the earpiece of the telephone receiver, coming back in distant stereo from somewhere in the air outside.

Another round drilled through the wall above his bed, a seascape falling like the flat blade of a guillotine, and Chan squirmed underneath the bed. Above him, muffled by the mattress and its box spring, he could hear the gunshots through the window and the telephone, as heavy bullets tore into his room.

And in the sudden, ringing silence that followed, he recognized the caller's voice, as if from miles away.

"I hope we understand each other, David. Tell the man. It just gets worse."

Chan felt the spreading wetness in his satin shorts and wondered how much worse a day could be.

6

"This white man. You could recognize him from a photograph?"

Across the desk, Sachiro Matsumoto nodded. "Certainly."

"But you have never seen his face before?"

"No, sir. He was a dark man, as I said. Perhaps Italian, but..."

Taoka waited for a moment, finally prodding his lieutenant. "Yes?"

Sachiro shook his head again. "I must apologize."

Taoka raised an open hand, the little finger missing from its first joint, just above the knuckle.

"Never mind," the Yakuza commander said. "He was a soldier, nothing more. His words are more important than his face. Repeat the message, please."

Sachiro straightened in his chair, a student making ready to recite before his class.

"He warned against intruding on established territories in America. He didn't mention drugs, but there was no mistaking his intention."

"A specific territory?"

"No, sir." Matsumoto's voice acquired an edge. "His comments made it clear that he was acting on behalf of Ho Yuan Lee."

"Explain."

"He said that China white should come from China. Some remark comparing sushi and an egg roll. Racist trash."

Taoka smiled. "I wonder. Have the problems at your flat been taken care of?"

"Yes, sir."

He could picture the disposal team at work, the corpses bundled into laundry baskets for removal, bloodstained carpet cleaned or lifted and replaced. It all cost money, but the price tag would be minor in comparison with having homicide detectives launch a full investigation of the family. Such probes were underway already, Taoka realized, but they were nibbling around the edges of his empire, going nowhere, while a shooting at his lieutenant's home would place them on the inside, one step closer to himself.

"Do you desire a change of residence?"

"No, sir."

The answer had been predetermined. Matsumoto would lose face if he sought shelter in a safehouse, his effectiveness and value to the family diminished by his distance from the action. Taoka had expected nothing less than selfless courage from his second-in-command.

"Security will be increased, of course," he added, satisfied when Matsumoto didn't smile or indicate relief. "You were informed about the other moves against us?"

"Yes."

"The yacht left no survivors, but we have descriptions of the man who damaged it. They conform to your description of the man at your apartment."

"It's war, then," Matsumoto said.

"Perhaps. It would be helpful, I believe, if we could first identify our enemy."

"The Triads, obviously."

Taoka frowned. "When have the Triads ever paid a white man to attack their enemies? Can you recall a single instance?"

Matsumoto shrugged. "Times change. If Lee is dealing with the mainland syndicate, they'd be happy to supply him with a man—or even with an army, if he made it worth their trouble."

"*We* are dealing with the mainland syndicate, Sachiro—or a portion of it. We mustn't be rash enough to launch a war against our friends by accident. Their goodwill is essential to the present enterprise."

"There must be some way to assign responsibility."

"Our contacts in Chicago and Nevada should be useful. Speak with them as soon as possible. Initiate inquiries. Make it understood that we're interested in peace and profit. If this brief unpleasantness is the result of a misunderstanding, we're anxious to resolve the problem to the benefit of all concerned."

"Misunderstanding?" Matsumoto's eyes were narrowed in confusion, anger showing through.

"A misperception. Bad advice. It's entirely possible that someone from Los Angeles, perhaps, or Florida, believes that we desire to take the food out of their mouths. In such a circumstance men often sacrifice their common sense and dignity through rash behavior."

"And if we identify the men responsible?"

There was a note of challenge in his lieutenant's voice, which Taoka chose to disregard.

"Then we make every effort to restore the peace. Vendettas are expensive, and they seldom turn a profit."

"We're all diminished if we tolerate such insults."

"Tolerance is useful in its place. The time will come when hostile moves against us are repaid in kind."

"And Lee?"

"He'll be dealt with if he's responsible for our embarrassment."

"You doubt it?"

"Chu Lien Pang isn't the only Triad family, and Ho Yuan Lee isn't our sole competitor from China. We accomplish nothing if we strike out aimlessly, without confirming targets in advance."

"Surveillance?"

Taoka nodded. "If he meets with the Americans I wish to be informed. His contacts shall be followed and identified. If Lee is found to be responsible for the attacks against our family, he'll be punished."

Finally Matsumoto smiled.

"That's all," Taoka told him, nodding in response as Matsumoto rose and bowed before leaving. Outside, he glimpsed a pair of sentries waiting in the corridor before the door was closed.

Taoka hated living under siege. It called up memories of Tokyo, the 1950s, when he was a young and reckless leader of the *gurentai*—black market gangsters who had flourished in the postwar occupation years, competing for the government's attention and approval with attacks on Communists and left-wing labor unions. Violence had been commonplace in those days, ragtag armies clashing in the streets and leaving broken bodies in their wake. When politics wasn't involved, the gangs fought one another over territories, mimicking the urban warfare that had scarred America in Prohibition. Taoka had been hunted by his enemies and driven underground, but he'd triumphed in the end, securing an alliance with the mighty Yamaguchi-gumi syndicate. Years later, when a group of his immediate superiors combined to organize Ichiwa-kai, Taoka had been ready to assume command of Honolulu, chosen on the basis of his record as a man who got things done.

Of course there'd been setbacks in his life, mistakes he'd been forced to reconcile. The missing pinky of his left hand had been sacrificed through *yobitsume*, the ritual finger-cutting practiced by Yakuza members in atonement for personal failure. Taoka's error—overlooking an informer in the ranks, resulting in a number of arrests and confiscation of a firearms shipment entering Japan—might easily have cost his rank, perhaps his life, among the mobsters of another country. Through his act of sacrifice and self-abasement, he demonstrated loyalty to the family and gave his promise to proceed without a repetition of his grave mistake.

It was a promise he'd kept for fifteen years. Among his fellows, Taoka was renowned for coolness under fire, his analytical response to daily problems and the extraordinary crises that arose from time to time. So far the various attacks against his family in Honolulu weren't Taoka's fault. Superiors at home couldn't blame him for any of the early losses in what seemed to be a shooting war.

What happened next, however, would be his responsibility, and his alone.

It was essential that he hold his troops in check until their enemy had been identified beyond the shadow of a doubt. A general assault upon the Chu Lien Pang society or any Triad, let alone the Mafia, could be disastrous. Members of the Yakuza were still outnumbered, highly vulnerable in America, and if the Triads went to war in Southeast Asia, business dealings would be jeopardized throughout the hemisphere. In that case, it would be Taoka's fault, and *yobitsume* wouldn't be enough to expiate his guilt.

It would mean *sepuku*—suicide.

Taoka lighted a cigarette, sat back and watched the smoke form lazy, abstract patterns as it rose.

Not yet.

He wasn't finished with his life, by any means. His enemies might kill him in the days to come if he grew careless or their numbers overwhelmed his family, but Taoka wouldn't stumble into battle like a drunken sumo wrestler, heaping one mistake upon another until he was forced to offer up his life in recompense.

The dying, he decided, would be left to others. To his enemies.

And they wouldn't have long to wait.

A MILE FROM TAOKA'S office in the heart of Honolulu's Chinatown, another early conference was convened that morning. Ho Yuan Lee presided in his role as local *shan chu*—literally, "hill chief"—of the Chu Lien Pang society. Across the spacious desk sat David Chan, Lee's second in command, and Benny Kapioliani, favored with an audience because his business—and a major stock of Triad contraband—had just gone up in flames.

"Repeat the caller's message," Lee commanded.

"He referred to the destruction of our warehouse," Chan replied. "It was described as punishment for trespass on a territory that is 'spoken for.' His words. And he made reference to the Matthews."

"Which you understood to mean..."

Lee knew the answer in advance, but he was testing Chan.

"The Mafia."

That brought a groan from Benny, and the fat Hawaiian shifted nervously.

"You have a comment, Benny?"

"Christ, the fucking Mafia."

"Or so the caller claims. It's an easy threat to make. In Hong Kong there are worms who pose as members of the Triad to obtain respect. We punish them from time to time."

"You didn't punish *this* guy," Benny blurted. "Jesus, we had two, three million dollars' worth of grass inside that warehouse, not to mention all the other fucking—"

"Language, Benny."

Kapiolani shut his mouth as if he'd been slapped across the face. Whatever might have happened at the warehouse, and whoever might have been responsible, his first concern was Ho Yuan Lee.

"I'm sorry."

"A reaction to the momentary stress. We understand, of course. But you'll need your wits about you, Benny. Self-control may often salvage hopeless situations. Discipline is everything."

"I understand."

Lee forced a smile, convinced that Benny understood no more than he could see and feel. The fat man was a primitive who let his appetites control his actions. Women, food and alcohol—together with the cash required to guarantee availability of same—comprised the limits of his world.

"The warehouse was insured," Lee said.

"A standard figure, sure. We had to, or we never would've got the lease. It won't come close to covering our losses on the grass and all the other shi—the stuff we lost."

"I understand that, Benny. Still, we may be thankful that the arsonists were thorough. If a portion of the hidden inventory had survived for a police investigation, some of us would face a greater difficulty than the simple loss of product."

Benny's glum expression left no doubt that he was clear on which of "us" would take the fall in case of any narco repercussions from the warehouse fire.

"I guess," he muttered.

"And we have a fair description of the man who vandalized our gaming room?"

"Big haole," the fat Hawaiian replied. "Nothing you could put a finger on, but he went through there like a pro."

"No robbery?"

"He didn't have the time," David Chan said. "However, with the smoke and gunshots, the police became involved."

Lee shrugged the statement off.

"The gambling is an open secret, amply covered by our payments to the vice squad. Drugs are something else entirely. With the pressure out of Washington, police may not feel free to look the other way."

"And if it *is* the Mafia?"

"Then our associates in New York City, San Francisco and Los Angeles will have an opportunity to help protect their mutual investment."

"If they aren't behind the move themselves," Chan said.

"Unlikely. You forget that the Americans aren't unlike ourselves, divided into so-called families with separate regions of authority. They seek to undermine one another constantly. It would be typical for one group to proceed on such a course without informing others, even in defiance of their so-called ruling council. Honor has no place among barbarians."

If Chan was moved to disagree he kept it to himself. "Taoka?" he inquired.

Lee frowned. "I haven't overlooked the possibility of Yakuza involvement. He's jealous of our progress on the

U.S. mainland, and I think he wouldn't hesitate to risk a war."

"Involving the Americans?"

"Perhaps without informing them of his intentions. Greedy men are easily misled with promises of easy victory."

"Taoka needs a lesson."

"First, we must be certain of our facts. Remember that the Chu Lien Pang have treaties with the Yakuza in Thailand, Singapore, the Philippines. Untimely action may prove detrimental to the larger needs of our society."

"Investigation, then?"

"By all means. We're well within our rights to ascertain the facts of our misfortune and respond accordingly. I'm sure the elders of the Yakuza could find no fault in self-defense."

"Unless they are responsible for Kenji's treachery."

"One hurdle at a time," Lee cautioned. "Drive the weasel from your garden first, before you concentrate on unseen tigers in the forest."

Chan accepted the rebuke with stoicism born of long experience. Beside him, Kapiolani had begun to sweat.

"So, what becomes of me and mine while this is going down?" the Hawaiian asked.

"You'll be taken care of, Benny. As a prized associate, your health is our concern."

"I never gave a thought to taking on the Mafia or anything like that."

"You have a fighter's reputation, Benny. After all that you've been through, a minor challenge shouldn't worry you."

"What kind of minor? Do you understand that these guys can make you disappear? Like you were never born, I mean. You wanna start a war with God?"

"Their reputation is exaggerated, and their glory days are past. You ought to read the papers, Benny. It would be an education for you. Everywhere the Mafia is losing ground—to prosecutions, the Colombians, our own incursions on the continent."

"They aren't dead, yet. You'd be crazy to treat those bruddas like they got no teeth."

"Your concern is touching, Benny. As for you, perhaps a small vacation. Nothing distant—we may need you, after all—but something to avoid police harassment for the next few days."

"I wouldn't mind."

"Can you arrange the details, David?"

"Done."

"And the investigation of Taoka?"

"It may take a day or two."

"As soon as possible. You understand that time is of the essence."

"Right. I'll push it."

"Tactfully."

"Of course."

"That's everything, I think. For now."

Chan held the door for Benny, a question in his eyes.

Lee shook his head. Not yet, he thought. Their front man was increasingly unstable, but he might be useful in the days to come. If nothing else, he could be used to take the fall if they were forced to move against Taoka and the Yakuza.

Lee hoped it wouldn't come to that. He felt no kindness toward the Japanese—ancestral hatred drilled into him by his parents from his childhood in the final months of World War II—but he could recognize a losing proposition when it threatened his investments in the business world. Suppression of a small competitor was one thing, but an all-out shooting war between substantial syndicates brought grief to all concerned. Police were forced to take official notice of the various combatants, payoffs notwithstanding, and illicit income suffered all around.

The last great war in Lee's experience had been a family feud between the Chu Lien Pang society and members of the Shih Hai Triad, over narco traffic in the Philippines. No less than seven hundred men were killed or wounded during eighteen months of conflict, with financial losses estimated in the millions as police and military forces staged a crackdown to suppress the fighting. Theoretically a clash between the Triads and the Yakuza could span the globe, 200,000 soldiers called to arms in Asia, North America and Western Europe.

Who would be the victor when the smoke cleared? Could there even *be* a winner, as the fighting drained combatant war chests and authorities cut off the source of future income?

Lee wasn't prepared to open up Pandora's box without authority from his superiors, and even then he was prepared to act with circumspection and restraint. If the Taoka faction was responsible for overnight attacks against the Chu Lien Pang, their brother Yakuza might well decide to sit the battle out, provided they could turn a profit on the deal. In such a fashion, Kenji's fatal error would be punished, while the other Japanese preserved their "face."

And then there was the Mafia.

If any clash between the Triads and the Yakuza was fraught with global risk, how much more serious would be the conflict with Sicilians and their allies added to the roster of belligerents? He pictured the United States, with inner-city neighborhoods laid waste by fierce guerrilla warfare, troops and federal marshals on patrol against the gangs.

Enough.

If someone was about to set the world on fire, it wouldn't be Ho Lee who struck the match. He was content to deal with problems in his own backyard and smother errant flames, instead of dousing them with gasoline.

His goal was peace, and after that, prosperity.

If it required a death or two along the way, so be it. But the Honolulu *shan chu* of the Chu Lien Pang would choose his targets carefully, removing them with surgical precision.

Starting at the top.

7

Following the sniper strike on David Chan, Mack Bolan took a respite from his labors, circling the neighborhood of Kapalman Heights until he found a working pay phone at a service station that had closed for renovations. Barring random taps—a theoretical concern that Bolan found statistically improbable—it was the best that he could do in terms of nailing down security.

Six hours difference made it nearly lunchtime in the capital. He dropped assorted coins and listened to their music, punching out a number he'd memorized. It was a private line, no operator or receptionist to screen the calls. If no one answered, he'd wait an hour and try again.

"Hello?"

Brognola's voice seemed undiminished by the distance, as rough and solid as a cinderblock.

"Aloha."

"Well, now."

"Shall I call you back?"

"Not necessary. I've been cleaning house. A little sweeping up to keep things nice and neat."

It was Brognola's way of telling Bolan that the lines were clear of taps, at least this morning. Unless the call was being intercepted on the trunk line, or at Bolan's end, they could converse in relative security. For all of that, the Executioner was cautious in his choice of words.

"I met your friend."

"How is he?"

"It was touch and go at first. A couple of his critics did their best to close the show."

"Which network?"

"A minority concern. They were going at it hammer and tongs when I arrived."

"You dealt with their concerns?"

"The problem has been laid to rest."

"My weatherman says you can look for storm clouds out your way."

"They're blowing up already. We've had damage here and there, and I expect more flurries later in the day."

"If you need any kind of weather gear—"

"I'll let you know," Bolan said. "In the meantime I've been looking into local sports. You wouldn't have a program handy, would you?"

"Nothing that I'd want to bet the farm on," Brognola replied. "The way it reads right now, New York and California have a deal on tap to play Taiwan, but they've been getting lots of static from the Brooklyn team. Las Vegas and Chicago lean toward Tokyo."

"The Southern league?"

"Those guys are playing wait-and-see. Whichever side brings home the pennant, they're prepared to sign."

"Should I expect to see a mainland team around the islands?"

"That's a tough one. Generally the feeling seems to be that East meets West when someone scores a run. If either of the foreign teams foul out, my guess would be they'll have to finish off the tournament alone."

"That helps."

"No guarantees," Brognola replied. "The players in this round are subject to change without notice."

"That's normal. Smart money says neither team takes home the cup."

"A pinch hitter could spoil things, I guess."

"He could try."

"It's a rough way to go, without backup."

"No time. I'd hate to see the game in extra innings."

"Either way, this wild card should be careful someone doesn't hit the batter."

"That's affirmative."

"You'll keep in touch?"

"If possible. Whichever way it goes, you'll have the finals by tomorrow at the latest."

"Watch yourself, okay?"

"I'll make a note."

He severed the connection, dropped another quarter in the slot and called a local number. Tommy Anders answered on the second ring.

"What's happening?" the warrior asked.

"Does Armageddon ring a bell? When you go out to shake a town, you really shake it, don't you?"

"Are they squealing?"

"Covering would be more like it. Fire inspectors and the suits from HPD are working overtime to cover your itinerary, but the big boys like to play it cool. So far, the paper trail leads back to dummy corporations, owned by other dummies, on and on. You know the drill."

"I'm not concerned about admissibility. I want the players jumping every time they see a shadow. When they start to make mistakes, we roll them up."

"You're on the way," said Anders. "Kenji's people have been burning up the line to Tokyo, plus calls to L.A., Frisco and the Apple. Lee's been on the line to Vegas and Taipei. Ma Bell must love you, guy."

"I made a call myself. The man in Wonderland thinks Lee and Kenji may get snubbed if they start begging reinforcements stateside."

"Fair-weather friends? I'm relieved."

"If he's right. On the off chance, we'll need to have eyes on the runway."

"No problem. Three airports besides Honolulu accept U.S. flights. Let me make a few calls, and I'll cover all four."

"You were talking a meet with some friends."

"Standing by. I can pull it together inside half an hour."

"Let's do it. I may need their input before I proceed."

Anders gave him an address, and Bolan agreed on a time before breaking the link. Moving back to the car, he could picture the comic in action, the calls going out. The airport surveillance should be simple enough, since any stateside shooters would arrive in groups—and probably by charter flights if they were in a hurry.

Bolan hoped Brognola's call was accurate regarding the mainland Mafia abstaining from a clash between the Triads and the Yakuza in Honolulu. Playing two sides off against each other was a tricky proposition, but a three-way game would more than triple Bolan's risk. This way, his first-line strategy—encouraging his chosen targets to believe the Mafia was siding with their opposition—would create suspicion in the ranks and, ideally produce some careless errors.

He was counting on reactions from his enemies to keep the ball in play. If Bolan had to do it all himself, the odds against success were drastically increased.

And now he had civilians to contend with.

Cruising toward the meet, alert to any sign that he was being tailed, the Executioner hoped that he could limit the involvement of civilians to a strictly noncombatant role.

In past campaigns the lines had often blurred, and Bolan carried memories of men and women sacrificed in the pursuance of his private war. On one hand, he couldn't deny the right—indeed, the duty—of a dedicated man or woman to resist the predators with force, but he was ever conscious of the price that losers paid in games of do-or-die. The average John Q. Citizen, however righteous his intent, was ill-prepared to deal with savages who cut their teeth on guns and dedicated every waking moment of their lives to wreaking havoc in society.

Sometimes it worked. But when it failed, in part or altogether, Bolan shouldered the responsibility for wasted lives and shattered dreams. It was a burden he'd carried from his first campaign against the Mafia, and it was always with him, coming back in dreams or an unguarded waking moment, haunting him with names and faces from the past—the hallowed dead who sanctified his war and kept him going. Bolan knew they harbored no resentment of his effort—every one of them had been a volunteer—but he was conscious of their presence all the same. One more incentive in the moments when his fighting spirit flagged.

The meeting point turned out to be a Chinese tearoom in Manoa Valley. The place was closed, but Bolan drove around back as he'd been directed, and a young man with a .38 revolver in his waistband passed him through. Across the threshold, Tommy Anders met him with a handshake and a cautious smile.

"All present and accounted for," the comic said.

"I'm after targets, names," the Executioner reminded him. "It's not recruiting time."

"Your call. Just hear them out."

The private dining room had been designed to handle parties of a dozen, more or less. With half that number waiting for him, there was room to spare, and Bolan had his pick of chairs as Anders made the introductions, using Bolan's frequent alias of "Mike Belasko."

Circling the table clockwise, Tommy introduced Wong Yau on Bolan's left. A well-dressed businessman of fifty-something years, the man was heavyset, with salt-and-pepper hair, a nearly seamless face and manicured hands. His son, named Andrew, wore a lightweight suit, his collar open, showing gold around his neck.

The lady on his left was a surprise. Late twenties, Bolan estimated, as Anders finished introducing him to Lisa Yau. She was a classic Asian beauty, with her raven hair worn long and straight, the barest touch of makeup on her face. No rings or other jewelry showed, and he pegged her as a student or woman with her eyes on a career. If Lisa's father was concerned about her deviation from tradition, he concealed it well.

On Bolan's right, Tsuyoshi Ino and Hideki Toshiro represented the Japanese community. Both men were middle-aged, with Ino seemingly the older of the two. They dressed conservatively, business suits and ties, each bowing slightly as their introduction was completed. Ino wore a crew cut, thinning on the crown, and gold-rimmed spectacles that magnified his eyes. Toshiro rarely spoke and never seemed to smile, but on occasion Bolan caught a flash of gold from one of his incisors.

Tommy Anders, in the role of host, selected Wong Yau to begin.

"We represent a part of the community that seldom speaks aloud," he said. "Tradition warns us that police are frequently corrupt, and foreigners—" he forced a smile "—are seldom interested in what the Chinese have to say."

"I'm here to listen," Bolan told him.

"You know something of the Triads?" Yau inquired.

"The basics. Sketchy background and the current stats."

"Outside of China, each community becomes a world unto itself. Authorities are frequently content to close their eyes, unless some difficulty moves beyond the bounds of Chinatown."

"In other words," his son declared, "we're yellow niggers."

"Andrew!"

Turning on his sister, Andrew Yau was warming to the battle. "Am I wrong? Don't tell me you believe these white men give a damn what happens to the little yellow people down in Chinatown. They're only interested in cutting off the flow of drugs before they hit the mainland and the white kids get a taste."

Although he understood the young man's anger and suspicion, Bolan had no time for a debate. "The Triads victimized your people for three hundred years before they got around to mine," he said. "If we agree they should be stopped, that makes us allies. Maybe we can help each other. If you'd rather they were left alone, at least don't slow me down."

"My son speaks rashly," Wong Yau said. "Each race produces outlaws, men who speak of honor while they rape and rob the innocent. I think true honor calls for decent men to form a common cause against their kind. I pray that we aren't too late."

"If you're alive it's not too late," the Executioner replied.

"Ho Lee collects a weekly 'tax' from Chinese businesses in Honolulu," Yau continued. "Merchants who refuse to pay have 'accidents.' A few have died, but most are left alive to carry on their business, so that Lee can claim his share. The poison that he sells was offered first to Chinese children, making some of them his slaves."

"The Yakuza are much the same," Tsuyoshi Ino interrupted, speaking softly. "In our ancient history, they are revered as revolutionary heroes—what the Europeans call a band of 'Robin Hoods.' In fact they prey on weakness, terrorizing merchants, selling helpless women in the foreign marketplace like cattle, terrorizing those who would resist. At home the politicians and police protect the syndicates and use them like a secret army to suppress the left."

"Free enterprise," Bolan said.

Around the world—in Asia, Western Europe, the United States—a common thread of strident anti-Communism ran through every major criminal confederation. Depending on the time and circumstances, "patriotic" gangsters had achieved alliances with ruling forces in America, Japan, Taiwan and China, France and Italy, Korea, Indonesia and the Philippines. When stripped of empty rhetoric, however, gangland patriots were no more interested in democracy than Stalin or Fidel. They were concerned with power, and accumulation of the wealth that placed that power in their hands.

"As Mr. Yau has said, our merchants, too, have suffered from extortion by their fellow countrymen. A few resist, and they become examples to the rest. Police seem helpless when they take the time to study our complaints at all. Of late it seems to many that our only hope lies in disposing of the Yakuza ourselves."

"And of the Triads."

Bolan frowned. "Your courage is an admirable trait," he said, "but common sense advises caution. In the field the Triads and the Yakuza each have around a hundred thousand men committed to their cause. Not all of those are soldiers, granted. Some of them are old, some keep the books, and many are accustomed to a world where anything they ask for is delivered on a silver tray, no questions asked. But when it comes to killing, they have armies on the street. With all respect a group of merchants—even several dozen—wouldn't last two days against the kind of force your enemies can organize.''

"And you propose to do it all alone?" Andrew Yau asked incredulously.

"I'm not about to spin you any fairy tales. Either way it goes, the Triads and the Yakuza will both survive. The best that anyone can do right here, right now, is make a start. Disrupt one operation at a time. Eliminate *this* problem and consolidate your gains before another comes along. Unless somebody hits the magic button and we all go up in smoke, don't look for any miracles or absolute solutions.''

"A beginning is important," Ino said. "Without it we can never hope to see the journey's end. Not for ourselves, or for our children's children.''

"A beginning," Wong Yau said in affirmation.

"And the rest of you agree?" Bolan asked.

Nodding heads around the table, Andrew Yau abstaining with a frown.

"All right," the warrior said at last. "First thing, I want to clarify the purpose of our meeting. I have a basic handle on the local gangs, their operations, but I need more inside information to complete the sweep and make it stick. I'm not recruiting vigilantes, and I don't expect your people to be fighting in the street with gunners who are bound to chew them up and spit them out.''

"In other words," Andrew Yau snapped, "we give, you take. We put our asses on the line, and you score all the touchdowns. When the smoke clears you fly back to haole land and leave us here to deal with anybody looking for revenge.''

"I don't tell fortunes," Bolan answered, "and won't pretend to tell you what may happen when the smoke clears. If we all come out the other side together I'll be leaving. You're exactly right. I'm not adopting anybody, and I damned sure haven't got the time to put down roots. Right now I'm offering my expertise. Beyond that I'm prepared to go ahead without your help if necessary. Either way, we're looking at a short-term common cause."

Tsuyoshi Ino cleared his throat. "And what of government assistance?"

Anders fielded that one. "Justice has a strike force working on the Yakuza and Triads as we speak. Quite frankly they've been hampered up to now by noncooperation from authorities in Tokyo, Taipei and other areas outside of U.S. jurisdiction. Likewise, Asian witnesses are hard to come by when arrests are made. A break in Honolulu, with your help, could turn the game around."

"And if you fail?" The question came from Lisa Yau, addressed to Bolan in a somber voice.

"No impact on the federal drive. We've shaken loose some bits and pieces of the syndicates already in the past few hours. Nothing that will put them out of business, but police have more to work with now than they had yesterday. This time tomorrow, I anticipate a local power vacuum at the top, with room for prosecutors to step in and do their thing."

"Ambitious plans," Andrew Yau said. "A single man, prepared to crush the Triads *and* the Yakuza in one day's time, when the police of three great nations haven't been successful in three hundred years."

"As I explained, I don't expect to crush the syndicates, or even cripple them. A flesh wound, maybe, in the scheme of things, but we can give the law a chance to do its job. A simple scratch can kill an elephant, if the infection spreads. Who knows? Resistance might catch on."

"We've been hiding in the shadows long enough," Tashiro said, addressing Bolan for the first time since their introduction. "It's shameful to retreat from such barbarians. For generations we've sacrificed our dignity. Today, some of us pledge our lives against the common enemy."

"I don't need cannon fodder," Bolan told him, "and I don't propose to share my plans with anyone who might be called upon to testify. You've all been through enough without a prosecution for withholding evidence. As far as I'm concerned, this meeting never happened. If you want to help me—if you want to help *yourselves*—I need the kind of information only you can offer."

"And in payment for your help?" Lisa Yau asked.

"No charge. If I planned on getting rich, I'd probably be working for the other side."

"An altruist?"

"A soldier, plain and simple," Bolan replied.

She plainly had her doubts, but Lisa kept them to herself.

"Are we agreed?" As Wong Yau spoke, he glanced around the table, studying each face in turn. With the exception of his son, the others nodded in compliance.

"I shall begin," Yau said. "Ho Lee has many agents in the city, many 'fronts,' as you might say. There's a shop on Maunakea Street...."

And so the litany began. By turns they poured out everything they knew about the Honolulu operations of the Triads and the Yakuza, reciting names, addresses and the details of a hundred unsolved crimes. With their permission Tommy Anders set a compact tape recorder in the middle of the table, using up both sides of three cassettes before they finished.

Bolan made himself relax, absorbing what he could, relying on the tape for any details that escaped his memory. He knew it was a start and wondered whether it would be enough.

8

The office on Pali Highway billed itself as a modeling agency, offering job placement at home and abroad. The tasteful Yellow Pages ad showed smiling faces, bright and wholesome, looking toward the future with delighted eyes. It didn't mention anything about the kind of future that selected clients could expect once they accepted one-way airline tickets to Japan, Korea or the Philippines.

Before he left his meeting at the teahouse, Bolan knew the agency was owned and operated by the Yakuza. While normal jobs in modeling were found for several dozen girls each year, the bulk of them employed in Honolulu, other "clients" were encouraged to expand their personal horizons, seeking out "adventure" and "romance" in the exotic Orient. There seemed to be no shortage of employment opportunities for models, hostesses, receptionists—but all of it boiled down to prostitution and pornography, with helpless women working for their masters in conditions that were more akin to slavery than free enterprise.

And Bolan knew the Yakuza's connection with the sleazy racket going in. Before the 1980s, tourists from Japan were rather easily divided into two main groups. In Western Europe and America the visitors arrived as families, with cameras in abundance, to enjoy themselves at theme parks, shopping malls, resort hotels. In Asia, though, the travelers were almost always male, and they arrived in packs, booked through specific travel agencies to take advantage of the teeming hookers in Manila, Bangkok, Seoul, Taiwan and Jakarta. Japanese "sex tours" became so notorious by 1981 that a series of carefully orchestrated protest demonstrations were timed to coincide with Prime Minister Zenko Suzuki's heavily publicized tour of Southeast Asia that June. Suzuki was moved by the expressions of public outrage, and new legislation combined with adverse publicity to sharply curtail the popular sex tours.

All of which taught the Yakuza whoremasters one thing: if planeloads of johns couldn't visit the women, then hookers would have to be found for the patrons at home.

Almost overnight the Asian flesh trade shifted into reverse, with women from various parts of the world imported for service in Japanese brothels and sex clubs. Some were purchased outright from their penniless families in Thailand and Indonesia, while others were recruited by subterfuge, lured to Japan with promises of glamorous employment, there "conditioned" with drugs, gang rape and other forms of abuse until their spirits were broken and the will to resist hammered out of their souls.

Within a decade Japan's fleshpots had made the Algerian slave marts obsolete, and Bolan welcomed the opportunity to pay back some of the suffering dished out by Yakuza pimps.

He found Trans-Global Modeling without a hitch, his circuit of the block complete in time to see a pair of young Hawaiian women exiting the office with brochures in hand. He parked downrange and watched them disappear around the corner, taking time to double-check the leather briefcase resting on the shotgun seat.

Inside, five pounds of C-4 plastic explosives had been evenly distributed around a battery and detonator, with a fistful of incendiary sticks thrown in to finish off the recipe. He set the timer to allow himself eight minutes, in and out, aware that it should take him roughly half that time if everything went well.

And if it didn't, well, at least the Honolulu blitz would finish with a bang.

He left the car unlocked, more interested in hasty exits than security just now, and crossed the street, approaching his selected target from the south. The double doors in front were automated, opening as Bolan's shadow broke the beam of an electric sensor. He stepped across the threshold into frosty air-conditioning, the gooseflesh rising on his arms despite the shirt and jacket that he wore.

The waiting room was empty, but a blond receptionist met Bolan with a smile most men would die for, leaning forward on her elbows to display a hint of cleavage as he crossed the room to stand before her desk.

"Good morning, sir, and welcome to Trans-Global. May I help you?"

Bolan palmed the Beretta, holding it where she could see the weapon as he placed the briefcase on her desk.

"Why don't you help yourself," he said. "My treat. Get out of here, and don't come back."

"But, I—"

"Right now!"

She bolted, scooping up a handbag on the run and leaving Bolan with the outer office to himself. Three doors confronted him, a rest room on the far side of the office and a pair marked Private, set behind the empty desk like bookends. The warrior chose the left on impulse, counting down the doomsday numbers as he made his move.

A swift kick snapped the latch, and he was across the threshold by the time the door rebounded from its impact with the wall. In front of him was another desk, without the smiling blonde.

The tenant of the office was a slender Japanese, his hair combed back to emphasize a high-rise forehead, an expression of surprise upon his face. The guy was plainly used to following a schedule, relying on subordinates to fend off unforeseen intrusions.

Still, the voice was clear and firm as he demanded, "Who are you? What do you want?"

"You're going out of business," Bolan told him, setting his loaded briefcase in the middle of the room.

"You can't be serious."

"One chance to walk away," he said, "and tell your people they should check their history. The slave trade's been illegal for a hundred years or so."

"I don't quite understand—"

"Wrong answer."

Bolan heard the others closing in behind him. There was no way of telling if his own explosive entry to the office had alerted them, or whether Mr. Clean had pressed a panic button. It hardly mattered either way. With something like a millisecond left in which to choose, he got off a round at the thin man and turned to face the troops.

Four gunners confronted him, two in front with automatic weapons. The Executioner now saw precisely what he would have found behind the second Private door. It struck him as peculiar that the agency would rate a four-man guard, and instinct told him that his blitz was having an effect. No time to think about it now, however, as he triggered two quick rounds in the direction of his enemies and scrambled toward the only decent cover in the room.

The lead man took his parabellums high and low, a throat wound and the other ripping through his groin. The little Ingram stuttergun went off without direction, chewing up the wall to Bolan's left before he reached the desk, a long dive clearing it with half an inch to spare.

The dead office manager broke Bolan's fall, one arm of his upended chair colliding painfully with the warrior's hip. He concentrated on the three surviving gunners, realizing *all* of them had submachine guns as they opened up in unison, a hail of bullets drumming on the hardwood desk and shattering the window at his back.

The window that was Bolan's only chance to save himself.

He took the time to check his watch. Two minutes left, and counting. If he figured half that time to stage his break, there might—just *might*—be time for him to clear the blast zone with a heartbeat left to spare.

Discarding caution, Bolan rolled the dead man from his capsized chair and propped him upright so that he was seated on the floor behind his desk, chin slumped against his lifeless chest. It would require coordination, perfect timing, but the Executioner had no choice. Without a decoy to distract the opposition, he was finished.

Wriggling behind the dead man, Bolan brought his knees up to his chest and braced both feet against the flaccid spine. He strained to grip the dead corpse's collar, hauling backward until it lay partially on top of him, back bowed, arms trailing on the floor. It wasn't perfect, but it was the best that he could do.

A final glance to peg the window's distance and position, as another burst of automatic fire cleaned out the last few shards of glass. Atop the desk, a bullet clipped the dead man's In tray, scattering his files and snapshots of prospective ''models.''

Bolan made his move, legs thrusting out like pistons, with the body taking flight. The guy sprang up from cover, flailing to the right, and rubber legs were folding under him when three converging streams of fire took over, spinning him around and waltzing him across the littered carpet, pinning him against the nearest wall.

The warrior moved before his opposition had a chance to recognize its critical mistake. He came up firing, the Beretta set for 3-round bursts, and he saw one of his assailants stagger, going down, before he reached the window on his second loping stride.

There was a courtyard just outside, a tiny square of lawn between the window and a fence that screened a narrow alleyway. A headlong dive took Bolan through the window, and he hit a flying shoulder roll before the two remaining SMGs corrected, emptying their magazines in an attempt to compensate. He used the time it took them to reload, legs pumping in a sprint before he hit the fence and vaulted over, scattering a row of trash cans as he landed on the other side.

The little sports car came from nowhere, screeching to a halt ten feet from Bolan as he struggled to his feet. A trap! Instinctively he leveled his Beretta at the windshield, finger tightening around the trigger in a flash before he recognized the face of Lisa Yau.

"Get in!" she snapped, and Bolan didn't argue, settling in the shotgun seat before she dropped the sportster into first and roared away.

Another pair of gunners were approaching the alley's mouth, but they'd come prepared to nail a man on foot. The car surprised them, and they broke to either side as Lisa held her course, accelerating through the gears. One of them raised a weapon as the sports car drew abreast, and Bolan hit him with a burst that punched him back against a Dumpster, crimson blotches stitched across his shirt and jacket as he fell.

The lady didn't use her brakes as they erupted from the alley, tortured rubber shrieking in response to angry horns around them. Somehow Lisa kept it on the road and found a slot in morning traffic, weaving in and out past slower cars. She'd traveled half a block when the explosion smothered traffic sounds.

"Sweet Jesus! What was that?"

He glanced behind them, watching smoke blot out the sky.

"An accident," he said.

"Oh, sure."

She veered across two lanes of traffic and caught a side street, Bolan watching for pursuers as she cut her speed to an approximation of the posted limit.

Gunners had been waiting for him, staking out the agency—and, by extension, other targets on his list, as well. The Executioner hadn't consulted anyone about his choice, and he accepted the conclusion that a similar reception would have greeted him at most—or all—of his intended stops.

His enemies were thinking logically, defending what they owned, but that didn't explain the lady's presence in a Honolulu alley under fire.

"Pull over," Bolan ordered after they had traveled better than a mile from Pali Highway.

"Here?"

He reached across to grip the wheel, with Lisa working on the clutch and brake to keep from cracking up against the curb. They coasted to a stop outside a neighborhood convenience store.

"I'm waiting," Bolan said.

"For what?"

"An explanation."

Lisa made a show of irritation. "I just saved your life. How quickly they forget."

"I'm not forgetting anything. You followed me."

"Of course. How else would I have found you?"

Bolan cursed his own distraction, so intent upon his target that he failed to check his back. In other circumstances such an error could have cost his life. It was an oversight that he wouldn't repeat.

"Still waiting."

"This is gratitude?"

"Suspicion," he corrected her. "You had a reason for the tail. Let's hear it."

"Curiosity?"

"No sale."

"All right, let's say I have a stake in what you're trying to accomplish. Maybe I don't feel like sitting back and watching from the sidelines while a stranger fights my battles for me."

"We agreed—"

"You made agreements with my father and the rest," she contradicted him. "If you recall, I never promised anything except the information you requested. No one asked me what I planned to do while you were out here slaying dragons."

Bolan frowned. "Your father said—"

"That none of his associates from Chinatown would interfere. I haven't, either—not unless you call a rescue interference."

"Damn it, Lisa...."

"Now you're angry. Honestly I could have let you die back there."

"My question's still the same," he told her, most of the initial anger bleeding from his tone.

"And so's my answer. I've been watching people duck and cover all my life. I'm sick to death of looking in my father's eyes and seeing fear each time he talks about the Triads. It seems to me that if I can't dredge up the nerve to take a stand, I might as well trade in my education for an apron. Either way, I'll wind up like my mother, tending house and hiding from the world."

"You sound more like your brother," Bolan said.

"Not quite. He lets the macho posturing get in his way sometimes, with all that talk of fighting back and his karate practice. Please don't get me wrong. I love him dearly, but he's no Bruce Lee."

"And you?"

It was the lady's turn to frown.

"I hadn't thought it through to that extent. This morning when I saw you were prepared to do the job yourself, and everybody else was satisfied to let you risk your life, I knew I couldn't wait to see what happened on the evening news."

"You could have been an item on your own."

"We made it, didn't we?"

"This time."

"Okay, then."

"Not okay. You know the enemy enough to hate him, and you've seen what he can do. It isn't good enough to blunder in on something like the set back there and pray for luck to see you out the other side. You're not prepared to fight this kind of war."

"Because of sex?"

The warrior shook his head, a flash of memory producing images of half a dozen lethal ladies in the time it took to answer Lisa's question.

"No," he said, "because you're not a killer."

Lisa seemed surprised by Bolan's answer. In another moment he could see the spark of recognition in her lovely almond eyes.

"I thought...oh, Jesus. All this time I didn't understand. Some kind of undercover cop, I told myself." The lady shook her head, as if in disbelief. "You weren't investigating anyone back there. You meant to kill them."

"Welcome to the war."

"That noise...an accident, you said. What was it really?"

Bolan held her eyes with his. "It was a slaver going out of business. One-on-one communication in the only language savages will ever understand."

"Who are you?"

"I'm a specialist. Sometimes when technicalities get in the way of justice I find alternate solutions for a problem."

"You're a vigilante."

"If you like. The truth is, Lisa, that I'm less concerned with labels than results."

"Ends justify the means?"

"Within established limits, yes."

"I guess I didn't mention that I graduate from law school at the end of next semester."

"Great. I have no quarrel with lawyers as a group. Some individuals let greed or rhetoric obscure the spirit of the law."

"And when they do, you're there to waste them, right?"

"They're not priority," he said. "Besides, it wouldn't leave me much free time."

"You're dangerous," the lady told him, nearly whispering.

"You're catching on."

"So, now what?"

"Now you drive."

9

A silent twenty-minute drive brought them to Mapuna-puna, where Lisa Yau dropped him at a car-rental office. Bolan watched her drive away before he went inside and used a set of fake ID to rent a compact car. Bolan's legs were cramped when he scrunched in behind the wheel, but he wouldn't be going far, and he could tolerate the minimal discomfort for the time it took to reach his waiting vehicle.

His thoughts went back to Lisa as he drove, with frequent aimless turns and one eye concentrating on the rental's rearview mirror. She'd followed him from their encounter at the teahouse, seemingly intent on helping Bolan with the mission, which she misperceived as an investigation by the federal government. Her plans from that point on were nebulous at best—hang out and watch, perhaps, or lend a hand with some impromptu testimony if "Belasko" needed any help.

Whatever, she clearly hadn't expected anything along the lines of what went down on Pali Highway. She wasn't a child, by any means, but Bolan would have bet the farm that guns and bombs were foreign to her world. A child of thrifty parents, soon to be a lawyer, she was better off than many of her people in the islands—or the States. She'd be used to seeing violence once removed, in books and movies, on the TV news.

And stumbling across reality could be a shock, no doubt about it.

Sometimes it was fatal.

Bolan had a hunch that Lisa Yau would manage to survive, but her reactions still concerned him. Would the revelation of his mission spark an angry scene between the woman and her father? Would she challenge Tommy Anders? Call the police?

The one thing he felt sure that Lisa wouldn't do was warn the Mob. However she might feel about his war, they shared a common enemy, and she'd been angry enough about the Triads to attend the teahouse meeting, sometimes offering a name or address when her father's memory appeared to fail. The problem would be Lisa's conscience, eating at her from the inside out, as she imagined scenes of bloodshed in the street. In the end, it might be more than she could cope with, but he'd have to take that chance.

His war was still on track, despite a brief diversion, and he dared not falter now.

He started spotting unmarked cruisers five blocks south of the incinerated trash heap where Trans-Global Modeling had once done business for the Yakuza. Routine procedure, trolling in the wake of a disaster, with the officers alert for any looters—or a bomber who might just be fool enough to hang around the fringes of the crime scene and admire his work.

A nearby restaurant was open, and he parked the rental in its lot, pretending interest in a curbside newspaper dispenser, finally doubling back in the direction of his car. It sat outside the barricades, against a curb where shattered glass from storefront windows had been swept up into piles.

He dawdled past the wreckage, feeling foot patrolmen check him out along the way, and he was ready when a bluesuit moved to intercept him at the car.

"Your vehicle?"

"Yes, sir," he answered, putting on a rueful smile.

The bluesuit studied Bolan and cocked a thumb across his shoulder toward the pile of rubble that had been Trans-Global. "You were here when that went down, I take it?"

"Right."

"I guess you heard the blast, then?"

"It was pretty hard to miss." Bolan raised a hand that trembled with conviction. "God, it almost knocked me down."

"You were outside?"

"Just parked the car, and I was walking back to drop some film off for developing." Now, it was Bolan's turn to cock a thumb behind him, thankful he had noticed the one-hour photo shop on the next corner. "All of a sudden, bang! You shoulda seen the glass and shit go flying. I've been down there drinking coffee ever since. I would've had a little something stronger, but I couldn't find a bar."

"Was that the only thing you heard? The bang, I mean?"

"What else?"

The uniform considered mentioning reports of gunfire and the blood—without a body—that forensics had discovered in the alleyway out back, but sharing with civilians went against the grain.

"Forget it. Since you're here, I need to take a look at your ID. Formalities, you understand."

"Sure thing."

He showed the phony California driver's license used to rent the compact earlier. The alias would click, a day or two from now, when they retrieved the missing rental car and ran a check of standard field interrogation records, but it wouldn't matter then.

"How long have you been on the island, Mr. Belasko?"

"My second day. I'm in the advertising game—some business cooking with a couple of the big hotels—but who can pass on taking pictures when you've got the beach and all right there? I'd never hear the end of it if I went back without a couple rolls of snapshots."

He could feel the bluesuit losing interest. After jotting down the information from his phony license, the patrolman gave it back.

"Be careful pulling out," he said. "We got a lot of rubberneckers, here, and trash all over the street."

"I will."

He put a mile behind him, going with the traffic's flow, before he let himself relax. So far, so good.

IT WAS A LONG DRIVE HOME for Lisa Yau. She stopped three times along the way, twice stepping from her car to wander aimlessly along the street, pretending interest in the various displays of clothes or jewelry. The items and their prices didn't register, and she paid no attention to pedestrians around her, sometimes staring at her own reflection in a polished window as she waited for solutions to present themselves.

Her father had deceived her, or had been deceived himself. The man who called himself Belasko was no more a federal officer than she was, and if *he* wasn't, then who, or what, was Tommy Anders?

She'd been suspicious from the start, unwilling to admit that part of her mistrust was founded on the comic's race. She hated prejudice, though it had never really touched her life, and Lisa was uncomfortable with the notion that she might suspect a man of evil on the basis of his skin color. Her parents would have disapproved, but if her father could be wrong about the comic, wrong about Belasko, wasn't she within her rights to question his advice on other matters?

Motive was the key. She knew that much from studying her law books and absorbing lectures on criminal procedure. If Anders and his violent friend desired to help her people, then at least they weren't enemies.

But could a law-abiding group of citizens afford such friends?

At what point would the stain of vigilante violence rub off on her father and his friends, her brother? On herself? Once conscious of the basic facts, could she escape responsibility for all that followed? Was she, even now, a culpable accessory to crimes that included homicide and arson?

A disturbing thought emerged from the unanswered questions. Suppose that Anders and Belasko *were* employees of the government. Then, what? Were all the crackpot theories of conspiracy within the FBI and CIA in fact correct? Was Washington responsible for fielding an assassin in Hawaii to attack the Triads and the Yakuza?

And what could Lisa do—what *should* she do—if that turned out to be the case?

So far she had no evidence connecting Mike Belasko with a major felony. The single shooting she'd witnessed was a case of self-defense, a member of the Triad shot while trying to commit a murder. As for the explosion, she supposed it *could* have been an accident, or something that the Chu Lien Pang had brought upon themselves. For all she knew, Belasko had surprised them in the act of making bombs for use against the Yakuza or merchants who refused to pay their "tax" in Chinatown.

She stopped herself, aware that she was reaching now. Belasko had been honest with her to a point. He made no bones about the fact that he was waging war against the syndicates.

Which brought her home again to the question of her father's knowledge and his culpability in any crimes the stranger might commit. How far would any of them go to break the chains of gangland servitude inherited from other generations?

More important, could she turn against her own to stop what she perceived as crimes in progress? Should she contact the authorities, or hold her tongue and let Belasko's war proceed? If Andrew learned about Belasko's militant approach, would he be tempted to enlist and thereby jeopardize his life?

The questions begged for answers, but she had none. Angry with herself for being indecisive, Lisa stalked back to her car and started home.

If nothing else she could attempt to find out what her father knew about his mainland "friends."

And she could try to keep them all from being jailed, or worse.

THE GUN SHOP on Kinau Street had a reputation as a "powder horn," suspected of selectively ignoring state and federal laws to satisfy the needs of special customers. At one time or another, the proprietor allegedly had dealt with hit men for specific pieces and arranged bulk orders for the syndicate. More recently he was believed to have set up export shipments for the Yakuza, providing arms and ammunition that would sell in Tokyo for many times their basic list price in America.

Hawaii was among the toughest states in terms of gun control, but local legislation couldn't hold a candle to restrictions in Japan. Accordingly, a simple .38 revolver might cost two or three thousand dollars on a Tokyo street corner, and black market ammunition typically sold for ten or fifteen dollars per round. A dealer short on scruples could become a millionaire by helping arm the Yakuza, collecting his percentage while the Mob skimmed off its chosen weapons, selling the remainder to associates around the fringes of the underworld. If some of the illicit weapons were recovered, linked with Mob assassinations and the like, why should the stateside dealer feel responsible?

He was a patriot, preserving basic freedoms, after all.

So far, the evidence required for an indictment and conviction of the shop's proprietor was lacking. Federal wiretaps had been briefly instituted some months back, but transcripts of the dealer's many business conversations turned up nothing usable, and the surveillance had been discontinued after several fruitless weeks. Another bid to infiltrate the pipeline with an undercover agent had gone awry when someone higher up allowed the word to leak. The agent was reported missing, whereabouts unknown.

But Bolan didn't need to build a case for court, and he had all the evidence he needed to convict the dealer, sentence him and carry out the verdict of a higher law.

Before he visited the powder horn that morning, the warrior hit a local pawnshop and acquired a suitcase, scarred from years of wear and tear, but still intact. He took it with him, empty, when he parked his car outside the gun store, glancing left and right along the street before he went inside.

"Can I help you?"

Bolan recognized the dealer from his various descriptions, taking time to note that they were all alone inside the shop.

"Could be."

"If there was something special . . ."

Bolan let him see the silencer-equipped Beretta, covering the dealer as he backtracked to reverse the Open sign and latch the door. No point in having browsers walk in off the street until he finished his appointed task.

"You're making a mistake," the dealer told him, glancing underneath the counter, where a gun would almost certainly be hidden, ready in the case of an emergency.

"Could be."

As Bolan spoke, he made his way around the counter, closing on the dealer, forcing him in the direction of a storeroom in the back.

"If you're after money I've got six or seven hundred in the register."

"I thought I'd take delivery on a little something special."

"Special?"

"Uzis," Bolan told him. "With suppressors, extra magazines and ammunition."

"I don't carry anything like that," the dealer answered, going pale. "This shop is straight."

"Too bad. I guess I'll have to kill you, then."

"Okay! Hang on a second, willya?"

Bolan made a show of glancing at his watch. "Time's up."

The arms supplier folded, pointing to a crate beneath his workbench.

"Under there."

"I'll let you do the honors."

Bolan kept his distance as the guy picked up a crowbar, dragged the crate into the middle of the floor and sprang the lid. Inside, six mini-Uzis nestled in a bed of rubber foam, their silencers and extra magazines each wrapped in bubble plastic to prevent the parts from making any sound or damaging one another when the case was moved.

"I'll take the hardware." Bolan handed him the empty suitcase. "You can keep the foam."

"Hey, thanks."

The dealer spent a moment lifting out the weapons and accessories, arranging them with almost loving care in Bolan's bag.

"The ammo, now."

"It's gonna weigh a fucking ton."

"I'll manage."

"Sure, okay."

It took two trips to clear the shelf reserved for parabellum ammunition, and the case was nearly full when Bolan's captive closed the latches, shifting it to stand upright.

"A fucking ton," he said again.

In fact the soldier knew that it was more like sixty pounds—the guns alone would tip the scales at nearly twenty-four—but he could handle it all right, as long as he wasn't required to run a wind sprint in the process.

"How's your memory?" he asked.

"I do okay."

"I've got a message for the buyer when he calls."

"I'm listening."

"You tell him Matthew thanks him for the hardware. Got it?"

"Matthew, right."

"If he decides he wants his toys back I'll arrange for personal delivery. The ammo, anyway."

"I hear you."

"Let's make sure."

The dealer gave it back to him verbatim, sweating now, despite the air-conditioning.

"You're leaving me with shit, you know that?"

"It's a chance you take. Feel free to call the HPD if it'll help."

"So funny I forgot to laugh."

"One thing."

"Just one? How lucky can I get?"

"Don't be a hero. If you try to stop me I'll just have to take you out and phone the message in myself."

"I ain't the hero type."

Outside, the day was getting warmer, and Bolan felt a sheen of perspiration on his forehead by the time he reached his car. With the suitcase stowed in back, he left the shop behind, proceeding toward his next appointment with the enemy.

Removal of the Uzis was a gesture for the most part, mention of the Matthews calculated to unnerve Taoka with the threat of Mafia involvement on the islands. If his hit-and-run campaign was unexpectedly prolonged—or if, reluctantly, he was compelled to call upon civilian ranks for help, at least the extra hardware would be available.

The warrior hoped it wouldn't come to that, for everybody's sake, but Bolan was accustomed to the unexpected cropping up and altering his best-laid plans.

It was a risk that every soldier faced in combat, butting heads with a surprise that might support the cause or blow up in his face. The best defense was constant motion, robbing opponents of a stationary target, striking them as frequently and painfully as possible.

Until they cried for peace, or none of them were left alive.

He knew the Oriental mobsters well enough to realize that none of them were criers, and with that in mind, his options narrowed down to one.

The death card.

It was Bolan's ace, his hole card, and he knew that it was time to give the enemy another peek.

To find out whether they would raise or fold.

10

The tourist maps list Honolulu's Smith Street as "depressed" when they depict the area at all. It is a casual warning to beware, and while the neighborhood doesn't compare with mainland ghettos, it's still the dark side of a city known for sunshine and the beaming smiles of happy natives.

The accidental tourist may not run afoul of thieves or other low-life predators on Smith Street, but he runs a decent chance. Primarily the victims are those residents who occupy the drab low-income housing, children playing in the street because they have no parks or yards, eventually running with this gang or that for self-defense, the brief illusion of control in what is otherwise a hopeless, dead-end life.

In human terms "depressed" means higher rates of street crime and disease, illiteracy, unemployment—all the ills, in short, that keep an area depressed while its inhabitants are weaned on dreams of breaking out and making something of themselves. A fair proportion ultimately make the move, determination and survival instincts keeping them in school, away from drugs and gangs. Smith Street produces doctors, lawyers, politicians, just like any other Honolulu neighborhood, but the survivors have a different tale to share when they have reached the other side.

Mack Bolan knew Smith Street by reputation and parked his rolling arsenal on Beretania, knowing that a short block makes a crucial difference for the teenage thugs and vandals who may pass their whole abbreviated lives without emerging from the neighborhood where they were born. To some of these kids, Waikiki was foreign territory. California, on the mainland, was the dark side of the moon.

He traveled light, encroaching on the Smith Street neighborhood, and he had made a point of dressing down, the flashy thousand-dollar suit replaced by something off the rack. It was the kind of suit a cop might wear, and in his pocket, Bolan packed a badge that he was hoping might survive a casual inspection by his enemies.

If all else failed, the 93-R in its shoulder rigging would be all the warrant and authority he needed for the move he had in mind.

Hawaiian vice, inevitably, has been molded and influenced by the foreign cultures that have used the islands as a crossroads in the past two centuries. The numbers racket was relatively late, taking root in ghetto neighborhoods of the United States long years before the Mafia discovered that a fortune could be made from dimes and nickels, moving in to cut out independent operators where they wouldn't fall in line. The shift took place from roughly 1930 through the early days of World War II, depending on the locale, but numbers only reached Hawaii in the early 1950s. Starting with the 1.5 percent of blacks who occupied the islands, it expanded to entice the natives with a dream of instant riches won from pocket change. Still smaller in Hawaii than in any major city on the mainland, numbers still raked in substantial income for the syndicate.

And when you bet your favorite number with a Honolulu runner, you were betting with the Triads.

Smith Street was the heart of numbers action for the city, and the Triad's Honolulu bank was situated there, its bankroll perfectly secure behind the Chinese Mob's sadistic reputation for repaying any injury with interest. Rumor had it that Hawaiian toughs had actually robbed the bank some years ago, but it was never verified, since members of the Triads made a point of shunning the police. It *was* known that a pair of mutilated bodies—young Hawaiian males—had been discovered near Aloha Tower right around that time, their injuries suggesting both had lived a grueling two days in captivity before their jailers ended it with point-blank bullets to the brain.

On Smith Street, lessons of that sort were never wasted. Every street tough with envy in his eyes and empty pockets in his jeans got the message, loud and clear.

Rip off the Triads and they rip *you* off, one raw appendage at a time.

Mack Bolan didn't plan to rob the numbers bank, exactly. He preferred to think of it as a withdrawal, and the badge would help him make it stick. While Ho Yuan Lee was shaking his informants for the latest information on a dirty cop with extra money on his hands, the cash would be invested in another phase of Bolan's island war.

Poetic justice, right.

It was a Bolan specialty.

Its fearsome reputation notwithstanding, Bolan knew the Smith Street numbers bank would have security in place. For all that the proprietors could tell, there might be someone on the street deranged enough to try another grab, and a display of muscle wasn't wasted if it got results.

A pair of heavyset Samoan bruisers met him at the door, both packing iron beneath their baggy flowered shirts. He let them see the badge, just long enough to crank their bushy eyebrows up a notch, and growled, "Let's see the man."

A dingy flight of stairs brought Bolan and his escort to the counting room, where bruiser number three stood watch—or, rather, sat watch—with his folding chair positioned so that it would block the door. Another flash of tin, some muttered words from one of Bolan's shadows, and the chair was moved, the plain door opened on command.

"What's this?"

The banker might have been an aging jockey or a stand-up comedian in the kind of nightclub where there isn't any cover on the patrons or the hostesses. An indeterminate mixed breed, he was the kind of "local color" that the Triads like to use as front men for their operations outside mainland Asia. And his snotty tone decided Bolan's angle of attack.

"It's payday," Bolan told his host, completing one more pass before he tucked the badge away for good. "You miss your weeklies, and they send a repo man. That's me."

"Somebody's yanking you," the man said indignantly. "We haven't missed a payment since we opened. Check downtown."

"I've *been* downtown. They *sent* me from downtown. You get the picture, douche bag?"

"Hey—"

"You wanna ante up, or shall we take a ride? You got gorillas packing heat here, and I'll bet my pension none of them has got a permit. Then there's gambling, right? I think the IRS might have some questions for you when they hear about the cash you keep on hand."

"Fuck this! I got the right to make a phone call."

Bolan's move was swift enough to startle everyone around him, rough enough to bruise the man's larynx as he wrapped one hand around his skinny throat and squeezed. The three Samoans never made a move.

"You make your phone calls from the station, guy. Right now, you've got the right to keep your mouth shut. I suggest you take advantage of it, if you're not a connoisseur of pain."

The banker nodded, wincing as the move put added pressure on his throat.

"The money?"

Another nod. Bolan smiled and shoved the pint-size hoodlum back a pace, one eye on the Samoans. Just in case.

"How much?"

"Well, there's the basic payment, plus your interest and the penalties for overdue delivery. How much you got?"

The guy considered lying, but he had to figure that his unexpected visitor could count. "Two hundred K. A little more, I think. We haven't finished counting yet."

"Don't bother," Bolan told him, grinning. "It'll give the vice boys something to do."

"You're not from vice?"

"I'm homicide." The grin turned frosty. "Over there we meet a better class of people."

"Yeah?"

"It's funny, though. One slip, and you can lose a case like that." He snapped his fingers, saw the man jump. "Unsolved, and nothing anyone can do about it. Makes you stop and think."

"About the money..."

"Take your time. Five minutes long enough?"

"No problem."

"If you've got a bag or something I could borrow..."

"Hey, no problem. Always happy to oblige."

"I tried to tell the guys you weren't a worthless little shit, like they were saying. Just your average, everyday misunderstanding, right?"

"I guess."

It took five minutes, plus, for two uneasy gofers to complete the task of packing bundled currency inside a medium-size gym bag. The warrior didn't mind, all things considered, and he even shook the banker's hand before he left.

"You'll need to call the man," he said before the two Samoans walked him back downstairs.

The banker looked as if his breakfast might come back to haunt him any second.

"Yeah."

"Make sure you tell him every action has an equal, opposite reaction. Just like outer space. You try and fuck somebody over in the business world, they fuck you back."

"I hear you."

"If he's got a beef, you tell him he can take it up with vice, downtown."

"Okay."

He left the bruisers at their post outside the busted bank, and walked back to his car. The Executioner was smiling by the time he got there, wondering how the banker would explain his grave mistake—or whether he would get the chance.

It made no difference, either way.

Obtaining ready cash from his opponents had been half the plan. Investing it to bring about their ultimate destruction was the other half.

And Bolan had a few ideas already.

Yes, indeed.

"I'M FOLLOWING the action," Tommy Anders said, surprised to find his hand was sweating where he held the telephone.

"It's not enough to *follow*," Hal Brognola answered, sounding angry and weary. "I need to know what Striker's doing in advance."

"Good luck. You ever try to track a cyclone? What he's doing at the moment would be turning Honolulu upside down. If you want the details I suppose we'll all just have to wait and see."

"The stateside crowd is getting jumpy," the big Fed informed him. "We're hearing rumbles from New York, L.A., Chicago, Vegas. A couple of the younger capos want to put some shooters in the air, protect their pharmaceutical investments."

"I assume you can discourage them."

"We're working on it. Customs might have something up their sleeve, but with a valid passport, if your basic hardass leaves his iron at home, we haven't got a lot to hold him on."

"I don't need lots of time," the comic said. "If Striker's running true to form, it ought to break tonight. Tomorrow at the latest."

"Ought to?"

"Hey, I don't read tea leaves," Anders snapped. "You know the guy as well as I do. Hell, you've known him longer. Has he ever played according to the rules?"

"His own," Brognola admitted.

"So, 'ought to' is the best that I can do right now. He's got a list of targets, and he's kicking ass. The game would seem to be divide and conquer, but I don't believe he'll risk a bloodbath in the streets."

"It may not be his call."

"Just keep the families covered, if you can. The rest of it is up for grabs."

THE SPEEDBOAT SOLD for close to sixty thousand, but a ten-percent down payment closed the deal, with paperwork obliging "Martin Blake" to pay installments for the next three years. His credit, as reflected in a scan of doctored records, was superb, and with the interest that would bump the price some twenty-six percent, he got no arguments about immediate delivery. The trailer was a rental, and a quarter-hour drive brought Bolan to Kewalo Basin, where a berth had been prepared.

Opening the trunk of his sedan, he transferred two fat duffel bags from the car to the speedboat, taking time to stow the extra cash before he locked the vehicle and armed the various security devices. No one had a make on Bolan's wheels, as far as he could tell, but he'd rather have the guns and cash go up in smoke than see them in hostile hands.

Departing from Kewalo, Bolan trailed the coastline west until he rounded Barbers Point. He cut the engines a hundred yards off-shore and waited for the enemy to show himself.

The rendezvous intelligence had been a tip from Tommy Anders, passed along by one of his informants on the street. A private pleasure craft, the *Southern Star*, was scheduled in today from Singapore—by way of Bangkok, Mindanao and Guam—with cargo in her hold that didn't have a prayer of passing customs. As it happened, a delivery on the high seas had been scheduled, with a Triad pickup team exchanging cash for heroin before the *Southern Star* reached port at Waikiki. A false alarm was set to draw the coast guard north toward Pokai Bay, and nothing should have interfered with the exchange.

Except for Bolan.

As he waited, he removed his chosen hardware from the canvas bags and double-checked the pieces. Two LAW rockets for the heavy punch, disposable bazookas that could stop a tank—or sink a yacht—within a hundred yards. For backup, he chose the effective combination of an M-16 assault rifle with an M-203 grenade launcher mounted below its foregrip, combining pinpoint automatic fire with the authoritative 40 mm kick of high explosives and incendiary rounds.

At half-past ten his glasses found the *Southern Star,* a glinting speck on the horizon, saving fuel and cruising with a favorable wind behind her sails. Another fifteen minutes, and a droning engine pierced the silence, wasplike. Bolan shifted in the driver's seat to spot a flashy launch, emerging from the cover of the coastline, moving swiftly toward the yacht on a collision course.

He let the smaller craft pass, two hundred yards away, before he fired up his engines and set off in pursuit. It didn't matter if they saw him. The pickup crew could run or stand and fight, but he'd have the slower *Southern Star* in either case.

One hundred fifty yards, and roughly twice that distance lay between the speed launch and the *Southern Star.* He rode the interceptor's wake, content to let them think that everything was running smoothly, right up to the moment that he rained on their parade.

When they'd cut the gap by half, the shotgun rider in the speed launch turned to stare at Bolan, lifting something to his face. It occurred to Bolan that a spotter on the yacht had tipped them off by walkie-talkie.

He used a foot to drag the squat LAW rockets closer, resting one hand on the rifle in his lap. Mere moments now, and there'd be nothing anyone could do to spoil the play.

The pickup team had guns, and one man was pumping out rounds, his shotgun sadly out of range. The M-16 had no such limitation, and the Executioner relinquished the controls just long enough to raise his piece and aim, a 3-round burst enough to drop the gunner in a sprawl.

He watched the launch veer sharply off its course, the pilot opting for discretion over valor, his surviving gunner rattling off an automatic burst from an Uzi or an MP-5. The parabellum rounds fell short by twenty yards, and Bolan passed them by, his full attention focused on the *Southern Star.*

He didn't know the men on board, or whether they were armed. It was enough for him to recognize that they were running China white for money, smuggling poison into the Aloha State.

With thirty yards to go, he pulled up short and left the engines idling, shifting to retrieve the nearest fiberglass bazooka. Three men on the deck were watching him, one through binoculars, and Bolan saw them scatter as he raised the rocket launcher to his shoulder, sighting on the wheelhouse.

One away.

Its impact rocked the *Southern Star* and left her listing hard to port, dark smoke boiling from the cabin. Bolan dropped the empty tube and raised its mate in time to see a couple of the smuggler's crewmen throw themselves across the rail.

Round two, and this time Bolan sighted on the waterline, a frothy geyser spurting up as the projectile blew on contact. Salvage divers might retrieve the skag if it was stored in watertight containers, but the sharks and coast guard were in charge from this point on.

He didn't wait to watch the boat go under. Cranking up the wheel, he powered through a turn that aimed his speedboat back toward Barbers Point. He was hauling back on the accelerator when he saw the launch returning for another pass.

Her pilot must have found his nerve, or else decided that he didn't dare return without avenging the destruction of his master's shipment. Bearing down on Bolan at a speed approaching forty knots, her white wake streaming out behind, the gunboat had a shooter standing in the prow, the pilot hunched at his controls like a demented kamikaze.

Bolan throttled down and raised the M-16, one finger tightening around the trigger as his adversary closed the gap. Still out of range, the hostile gunner opened up with everything he had, the little stuttergun's defiant chatter nearly lost in so much open space.

The warrior took the shooter first, a short burst at the outer limit of the SMG's effective range, and saw his target tumble back against the pilot's windscreen. Instantly, before the pilot had a chance to drag the corpse aside or change his course, a high-explosive round was on its way from Bolan's launcher, dropping in on target with a simulated thunderclap.

The next split second brought the action of an old cartoon to mind, the gunboat stopping dead as if its prow had crashed into a stout, invisible brick wall. The engines kept on churning all the same, and in another heartbeat Bolan saw the vessel standing on its crumpled nose, a ball of flame devouring the foredeck, licking out to claim the pilot's seat.

Another instant, and the fuel tanks detonated in a secondary blast that scattered flaming gasoline and pieces of the shattered hull in all directions. On the shore, if anyone was watching, it would take perhaps a minute for a phone call to the coast guard, two or three to modify the general orders for a run to Pokai Bay.

The Executioner would be gone before the cavalry arrived, and if they found survivors from the *Southern Star,* he wouldn't mind. The message had been passed along, and he could drop the speedboat at Kewalo. It had served its purpose, and the dealer would recover it in time. If not he was undoubtedly insured.

The Triads would be mulling over Bolan's lesson for a while, and it was time to give the opposition equal time.

In war, like charity, it was more blessed to deliver than receive.

Taoka's family was about to take delivery on a taste of hell on earth.

11

When Lisa reached the suite of offices in Chinatown, she went directly to see her father, brushing past his secretary, entering without the customary knock. His first expression of surprise changed swiftly into curiosity and fatherly concern, as he beheld the grim expression on her face.

"What is it, Lisa?"

"May we speak in private?"

Sam Jiangsu, her father's friend of twenty years and junior partner in a chain of business enterprises, smiled and made a show of understanding.

"Family matters take priority," he said, already rising from his chair before Wong Yau could argue. Lisa stepped aside and gave him ample room to pass as he removed himself.

"Your rudeness, daughter?"

"Sam will understand. Sam *always* understands."

It would have been unfair to say she hated Sam Jiangsu, but Lisa neither liked nor trusted him. She did hate his reaction to her presence in a room—eyes that seemed to roam around her body like a pair of searching hands, the way he always seemed to lick his lips before he spoke to her, as if he were imagining her flavor. The man was nearly old enough to be her father, but he acted like a lovesick schoolboy... or a lecherous old man.

"Please, be seated. Tell me what has troubled you."

"Tommy Anders."

"Yes?"

"Have you examined his credentials, Father?"

"I believe we had this conversation once before."

"I know, but it seems that things have changed."

"Belasko." It wasn't a question.

"Yes."

"We asked for help. It has arrived."

"You *know* about Belasko?"

Her father's curiosity turned to confusion. "You were present at the meeting," he replied. "We know that he has worked with Mr. Anders in the past. He has the confidence of men in Washington."

"What kind of work? What men in Washington?"

Her father frowned and spread his hands. "Such things are often left unspoken. There are lives at stake."

"Our lives. If there is war in the community, *we* suffer most."

"The war exists. It didn't start with Anders or Belasko."

"Will it end with them?"

"Perhaps."

"And what if their attempts to help us only make things worse?"

"You voiced no such concerns this morning when we all sat down together."

"Things have changed."

"How so?"

"There have been . . . other incidents."

"Trans-Global Modeling," he said, surprising her. "The enterprise was a disgrace. It won't be missed."

"You knew?"

"About the bomb? Toshiro called. I was discussing it with Sam when you arrived."

"Belasko was involved."

It worried Lisa that her father didn't seem surprised. Instead he asked, "How do you know?"

"I saw him. I was there. He had a gun, and—"

"Policemen carry guns," her father chided. "Sometimes they're forced to use them. More in the United States than in our home."

She'd been born in Honolulu, but he always spoke of China as "our home," as if she'd been carried from the old world as a child.

"He isn't a policeman," she replied. "I think—"

Her father raised a hand for silence. "Say no more. It was unwise of me to let you have a part in this. Your own mistake was following Belasko."

"*My* mistake? I don't—"

"Be silent! Do you take your father for a fool? You think that I request the help of strangers and permit their actions to disrupt our lives? Before I spoke at length with Mr. Anders, inquiries were made. I still have contacts on the mainland. They, in turn, have friends in Washington. I was assured that Anders is reliable. As for Belasko... If his methods are effective, they may help preserve our way of life."

"I don't believe you're saying this. You always taught me to respect the law."

"It is a noble calling, and I know that you will serve it well," her father said. "But every system has its limitations, weaknesses. Today a murderer is sentenced for his crime and waits ten years before another court decides his punishment is too severe. Corruption is a fact of life—the petty bribes that keep society in motion—but today the plague of drugs affects us all. Our future is polluted by a handful of barbarians."

"You knew what he was planning all along."

"I have consulted Ino, Toshiro and several others. We agree in principle. Some ailments call for drastic measures to effect a cure."

"Suppose your cure is worse than the disease?"

"Impossible."

"You spoke of 'others.' I assume that you've shared your plans with Sam Jiangsu?"

Her father's smile was almost wistful. "Sam has been my friend since you were born. He helped me to survive your mother's death. I haven't burdened him with this, because our business may require a guiding hand someday besides my own."

She read between the lines and felt a sudden chill.

"You mean if something happens."

"Something always happens. No man is immortal, Lisa. I've made provisions for you and your brother, of course, but Sam is better suited to maintain the business. You have other plans, and Andrew... Well, in many ways he's a child."

It stunned her, sharing a discussion of her father's death as if the date had been arranged, and Lisa felt tears welling in her eyes. She realized that there was nothing she could say to change her father's mind.

His hopes and his survival had been staked on Tommy Anders and the man who called himself Belasko. Any steps she took to hamper them might spell disaster for the man who gave her life.

But if she couldn't stop them, could she help in any way?

Perhaps, if she could reach Belasko one more time...

And failing that, the only choice for Lisa Yau would be to stand beside her family to the bitter end, whatever that might be.

She had a premonition that the answer wouldn't be delayed for long.

THE TAPE RECORDER was concealed inside his desk, voice-activated, to record all conversations taking place in Wong Yau's office down the hall. On busy days—and there were many of them lately—Sam Jiangsu was forced to change cassettes with frequency, reviewing dialogues in private to determine which tapes he should save and which could be erased. The system had its drawbacks—he could only hear one side of conversations on the telephone, for instance—but it served him and the men who pulled his strings well enough.

Jiangsu's personal affiliation with the Chu Lien Pang society had cast him in the role of an informer. He wasn't a member of the Triads, but he knew them well enough... and *they* knew *him*. It would be accurate to say that Ho Yuan Lee maintained an open file on every Chinese businessman in Honolulu, information gathered on their families, their strengths and weaknesses, which might be useful to the syndicate. Some passed their lives with no more contact from the Triads than the weekly payments made for "fire insurance" or protection from the violent teenage gangs. In other cases, businesses were targeted for infiltration and absorption by the Mob.

And then there were the chosen few like Sam Jiangsu.

It had been sex, initially, that trapped him in the spider's web. A lifelong bachelor, Jiangsu enjoyed the company of girls below the age of thirteen years. His passion for their prepubescent bodies had been exercised discreetly, for the most part, but the Chu Lien Pang had ways of finding out a weak man's darkest secrets and turning them against him in the end. One afternoon a set of photographs arrived by mail, a phone call following to make arrangements for a private meeting. Face-to-face the ultimatum was delivered—serve the Triads as required, or face exposure and the ultimate disgrace.

Jiangsu served.

At first the price hadn't seemed very high. No money was demanded, and he wasn't asked to deal in contraband. The Chu Lien Pang showed no apparent interest in devouring the chain of restaurants he had established with Wong Yau. They merely wanted information now and then. More often *now*, since certain leaders of the Chinese community had worked up nerve enough to buck the Triads.

Not that any true resistance had been offered until now. Discussions had been held, their substance dutifully relayed by Sam Jiangsu. The Triad representative listened, sometimes taking notes, and smiled when he was finished. There'd been no action in reprisal, nothing to suggest that Jiangsu was jeopardizing lifelong friends.

The tape recorder was a relatively new development, "suggested" by his contact in the Chu Lien Pang, delivered—with instructions—at a meeting nine months earlier. Jiangsu had been nervous when he dropped by after business hours to install the microphone, concealing it beneath Yau's desk where even the most zealous cleaning woman wouldn't find it.

And there was guilt.

Somehow the act of taping Yau seemed worse—more treacherous—than simply echoing his conversations, passing on a summary of comments to the Chu Lien Pang. Before the tapes, Jiangsu had an opportunity to censor Yau's remarks and tone them down when he was critical of the society and its collectors, but recordings could be damning in themselves. Like photographs, they left out nothing. Blemishes—for threats—were obvious to anyone, and Jiangsu was sometimes worried for his friend.

Of late Yau had grown more stubborn in resistance to the Triads. He'd pay the weekly tax, of course—it was financial suicide to stop the payments—but it seemed he spoke more openly against the Chu Lien Pang each day.

Because he thought that he was speaking only to a trusted friend.

So far the Triads had been willing to ignore his insolence, but now...

The latest tapes were something else.

Yau's phone calls were bad enough. Disjointed monologues, they still revealed that he'd moved beyond the realm of mere complaints toward action that would place him on a hard collision course with Ho Yuan Lee. The white man, Tommy Anders, had encouraged Yau's resistance, and his name had been relayed by Jiangsu.

The Chu Lien Pang had failed so far in their attempts to neutralize Anders, and now there was another white man on the scene. The last tape made that clear to Jiangsu, and it would doubtless stir a furious reaction from the Triads. Yau had moved to a state of open war, and he'd done it all without the counsel of his oldest, closest friend.

It was absurd for Jiangsu to feel betrayed, all things considered, but he still couldn't deny a stab of irritation— even jealousy—when he imagined Yau discussing secret plans with strangers. Worse, with white men and the Japanese. He'd deliberately avoided Jiangsu, as if he knew about his old friend's treachery.

Impossible.

If Yau had found the microphone it would have been destroyed by now. His dialogue with Lisa had suggested that the silence was designed for Jiangsu's protection, to insure against retaliation by the syndicate, but could it be the truth? With time, Jiangsu's own duplicity had fostered paranoia, to the point that he imagined others to be guilty of his own transgressions.

Never mind.

Whatever Yau's intentions, Jiangsu had taken out his own insurance with the Chu Lien Pang. When Yau was finally dealt with—as he must be, soon—the Triads would remember who had served them well. The junior partner would inherit everything, and he'd shed the burden of informing on his dearest friend.

His late, lamented friend.

But first he had to make delivery on the latest tape. Its contents were explosive, and he knew the Chu Lien Pang's reaction would be swift, decisive. Ho Yuan Lee wouldn't ignore such treachery in Chinatown.

To save his own life, Sam Jiangsu must offer up another.

Just as long as he wasn't required to carry out the sacrifice himself.

ANOTHER WHITE MAN? Even after listening to Wong Yau's voice on tape, Ho Lee was skeptical. In his experience the typical Chinese wasn't inclined to trust strangers, much less members of a race that had exploited and abused them through the centuries. All rhetoric about the "melting pot" aside, his people had long memories. They grew up on a history of racist violence and invasions, opium wars and restrictive immigration laws, effective relegation of their fathers to the mines and railroads, restaurants and laundries. Dealing with a white man in the business world was one thing; trusting him with life and loved ones was a different thing entirely, and it went against the grain.

Which didn't mean Wong Yau was innocent, by any means.

His treachery was uncontested, captured on the tape for all to hear. The punishment was predetermined by his crime.

But first Yau would be called upon to rectify the damage he'd done by introducing strangers to the secret workings of the Chu Lien Pang society. One effort to eliminate the comic, Tommy Anders, had already cost the Triads several men, but he wouldn't escape a second time. Wong Yau would see to that.

And this Belasko—federal officer or hired assassin—would be dealt with simultaneously, as an object lesson to the white man's government.

In future they'd hesitate before they tampered with tradition.

Ho Yuan Lee considered ways and means of forcing Yau's cooperation in the execution of his allies. It wouldn't be easy—Yau wasn't a child to be intimidated by a simple threat against his life—but there were ways for such a thing to be accomplished.

Through his family, for example.

Lee punched a button on the desktop intercom to summon David Chan. A moment later his lieutenant stood before him, waiting for instructions. The man smiled as his boss explained what must be done.

Simplicity itself, yet the move would be a master stroke. Wong Yau would kneel before him as the peasants always did, once pressure was applied in the right places.

Before he finished issuing instructions to his second in command, the Triad chief had already revised the crucial last phase of his plan. While Tommy Anders could be executed outright, Lee had other uses for the warrior—this

Belasko. He could use a man of courage and determination, even if his skin was white.

Against the Yakuza, perhaps.

And in the process he could head off any ugly rumors of his own involvement in a Honolulu gang war. If Taoka's troops were decimated by a white man—working for the government, no less—it was impossible for anyone in Tokyo to blame the Chu Lien Pang society.

Instead of killing Mike Belasko, Lee would offer him a choice: continue his assault against the Yakuza, while sparing Triad targets, and preserve the lives of those whom he professed to serve. A clever soldier might see through the ruse, but if he suffered from the weakness of compassion, there was still a chance.

And if he balked, he would be killed. The perfect answer to a seemingly insoluble dilemma.

Watching Chan retreat, the Triad chief allowed himself a smile. It didn't fit his features, adding neither light nor warmth to Lee's expression, and it vanished in an instant, like a peel of laughter accidentally uttered at a funeral.

Ho Lee wasn't without his virtues—strength and courage chief among them—but he had no sense of humor. Jokes were wasted on him, though he sometimes laughed mechanically with his superiors to be polite. His life was serious, and even triumph was a cause for introspection, as he looked for ways to make the next win swifter, easier, less costly for himself and more expensive for his enemies.

This time he was convinced that he'd done enough. The plan was seamless, perfect. Short of intervention by the gods, it couldn't fail.

With that in mind, he settled back and thought of ways to make it better yet. The gods couldn't be trusted, after all.

12

The problem, Lisa Yau told herself, was finding Mike Belasko in a city sprawling over six hundred square miles, with 375,000 year-round residents and four to five times as many tourists. Looking for a needle in a haystack would be child's play by comparison, and with the list of targets her father and the others had provided, she couldn't be certain he'd even stay in Honolulu.

Still, she had the list and that was something. Precious little, to be sure, but she wouldn't be groping wholly in the dark.

Her choice had finally come down to one of loyalty, to her father and her people. She could blow the whistle on Belasko and attempt to have him jailed—provided that his federal sponsors didn't run a fix—but any such attempt would see her father charged as an accessory. Beyond that risk she also feared that a betrayal of Belasko and her father might allow the Chu Lien Pang society to tighten its control of Chinatown.

Which left her with a choice of pitching in or standing on the sidelines waiting. Neither option was attractive, but she knew that guilt would stalk her to her grave if she allowed her father to be swept away by circumstance while she did nothing.

So the problem was resolved. All she had to do was find one man in several million and assist him—somehow—in his hopeless war against the Mob.

She ran the mental checklist and began to hit the major targets, painfully aware that she could cruise the streets for days without encountering Belasko. Trailing him to a selected target had been one thing, but a chance encounter, culled from a potential list of over thirty strike points, strained the bounds of credibility. Without precision timing, she'd never know if she'd crossed his path or missed him by a mile.

But it was still the only way to go.

She could enlist an ally, but the range of choices was distinctly limited. Her father made no secret of his wish for Lisa to remain out of the struggle, and she wouldn't risk her brother, even if he knew the truth about Belasko's plans.

She thought of Sam Jiangsu and frowned, imagining a bad taste in her mouth. He'd been huddled in discussion with her father when she interrupted them that morning, and she hadn't been convinced by protestations of his ignorance. It stood to reason that her father's closest friend and business partner would be privy to a plan that threatened everything that they had worked for through the years. Sam *had* to know the truth.

And he'd be informed of Mike Belasko's moves against the enemy—if not beforehand, then at least a short time after they occurred. She'd be points ahead if she could track Belasko by his strikes as they took place, instead of waiting for a thirty-second wrap-up on the evening news. A pattern might emerge, and Lisa stood a chance of intercepting him at some point between engagements.

Why?

To offer him advice, a local's knowledge of the territory and the men he had selected as his enemies. Because she had no other bright ideas.

The details would supply themselves with any luck at all. Her first priority was making contact, and for that she needed help.

She needed Sam Jiangsu.

A simple call, no need to see him in the flesh if he agreed to help her. If he argued she'd use her own persuasive skills to make him understand the greater risks involved.

For good or ill her father was committed to Belasko, and the man's failure would inevitably spell disaster for them all. If Wong Yau went to jail, or worse, the Triads would devour his business overnight, and Sam Jiangsu would have a choice of bailing out—his life a waste—or serving at the pleasure of the syndicate until they shunted him aside.

She hoped the argument would wash, and realized that it was all she had. Sam would agree to help her or he wouldn't. If he failed her, all was lost.

She spied a pay phone on the wrong side of the street and found a hole in traffic, making an illegal U-turn in the middle of the block.

A simple phone call.

Yes or no.

Belasko wouldn't welcome her assistance, but she thought that he was smart enough to take advantage of experience. He wouldn't like it, but he would accept her to help because she gave him no alternative.

The options were unthinkable.

MOST DAYS the leader of the Yakuza in Honolulu was a reasonably happy man. He lived a life of luxury, with women at his beck and call, a private army at his personal disposal, ready to eliminate his enemies upon command. At home his various superiors seemed pleased with his performance and the eastward flow of cash that he maintained. His life was satisfactory.

Until today.

Since dawn, that life had been unraveling, as unseen enemies attacked on every side.

Unseen, but not unknown.

Kenji Taoka knew precisely what was happening around him, even though he seemed unable to reverse the tide. The Chu Lien Pang society had formed a treacherous alliance with a faction of the mainland Mafia to undercut his recent progress in the sale of heroin and other drugs abroad.

If he wasn't extremely cautious Taoka knew that all his hopes and dreams might lie in ruins by tomorrow—if he lived that long.

In Tokyo the master of his family—the *oyabun*—wasn't amused by late events in Honolulu. Orders had been issued by the ruler of the clan, and Taoka pledged to see them carried out or die in the attempt. No middle ground existed in the Yakuza when cash and honor were at stake.

The implications of a war against the Chu Lien Pang—perhaps against the Mafia or Triads as a whole—had been discussed at home, and the decision was unanimous. Aggression on the part of Ho Yuan Lee must be resisted with sufficient force to stabilize the situation and eliminate potential danger, while the *oyabun* and his advisers coped with any problems on a broader scale.

All Taoka had to do was fight the local war and make damned certain that he won. Capitulation was unthinkable to his superiors, defeat the kiss of death.

His death.

Accordingly Taoka had rescinded orders for a mere surveillance of the Chu Lien Pang, selecting the elite among his soldiers to prepare an armed response. It might take hours—even days—to finalize the plan, but he'd see it through. Ho Lee and his immediate subordinates were marked, and there was nothing they could do to save themselves.

Or was there?

Tracing Lee's accomplice in the early raids had been a problem, still unsolved. The Mafia had several hundred soldiers in New York and California, where the Chu Lien Pang were strongest, and the man—or men—who had been glimpsed in various attacks might never be identified. In fact the name meant nothing to Taoka, but he had to neutralize his enemy's most potent weapon soon, before the damage suffered by his own conglomerate became irreparable.

His only hope appeared to lie in the reports of similar attacks against the Chu Lien Pang society in Honolulu. Taoka knew his own men weren't responsible, in spite of provocation, and the raids left crucial questions glaringly unanswered.

Was the Mafia, in fact, betraying both the Yakuza and Triads in a twisted scheme to claim the narco traffic for itself? Were other, unknown forces somehow implicated in the game?

So far Taoka had no viable solutions. In the crunch he'd rely upon unexplained attacks to occupy Ho Lee, distract him while Taoka slipped a noose around his neck.

And if a subsequent investigation proved that Lee wasn't responsible?

Too bad.

The Chu Lien Pang had been a thorn in his side for years, and he was thankful for the chance to shake them off. No one could blame him for suspecting Ho Yuan Lee in the attacks. His own reprisal would be made on the direct instructions of his *oyabun*, an order that he dared not disobey.

It would be perfect.

All he had to do was find his target, line it up and knock it down.

Before somebody did the same to him.

THE PORNO STUDIO was situated in a spacious ranch-style home just off Pahoa, near the Waialee Country Club. It was a neighborhood accustomed to conspicuous consumption, flashy cars, and parties that began or ended at peculiar hours. More importantly the neighbors cherished privacy, and no one was inclined to ask about the changing shifts of men and women who arrived and left with no apparent schedule, day and night. As long as there was no commotion, nothing to require police assistance, it was see-no-evil, hear-no-evil all the way.

Except for Bolan.

He'd gleaned the address from his list of targets, moving back and forth across the city in a random search for prey, deliberately avoiding any sort of pattern that would make his moves predictable. By sheer coincidence the porno racket was a Yakuza concern, but he wasn't averse to burning Taoka's fingers twice in quick succession.

Nothing like driving a point home.

His dark sedan was slightly out of place among the Jaguar and Mercedes class, but Bolan didn't plan on staying long enough for it to register with any of the neighbors. In and out would do just fine, another strike to cost the Mob a few more hundred thousands, and he would be on his way.

To yet another target.

Parking at the curb, he double-checked the 93-R's load from habit, picking up a satchel from the shotgun seat before he left the car. Once more he trusted in the neighborhood and left his door unlocked. A car thief dumb enough to work Pahoa and environs wouldn't be the kind to settle for a midrange four-door when the cream of foreign and domestic rolling stock was at his fingertips.

The satchel, rather like a doctor's bag, made Bolan look official as he moved along the flagstone walk and punched the doorbell. One hand slid inside his open jacket, palming the Beretta as the latch was opened from within.

A sallow face regarded him with frank suspicion, changing in an instant to surprise and terror as he raised the pistol.

"Back."

The doorman followed orders like a natural, and Bolan used a heel to close the door behind him once inside.

"Let's see the man."

The gaping dimwit found his voice in time to say, "He's working."

"Well, I guess we'll have to interrupt him, won't we?"

"Yeah, I guess."

They crossed a sunken living room that doubtless proved ideal for party scenes. Bolan trailed his escort down a hallway to his left, the doorman pausing on the threshold of a bedroom two doors down.

"You're gonna piss him off."

"I'll take the chance."

His hostage didn't bother knocking. On the far side of the door, klieg lights were heating up the room, spaced out around a king-size bed where two young women were engaged in servicing a naked man. The cameras rolled, recording every precious moment for posterity.

The man in charge was tall and badly overweight, his beard in need of trimming, but he dressed like a director, from the cocked beret to Gucci loafers, wearing shades against the glare of the klieg lights.

"You crazy, man? We're working here."

"Take five," Bolan said, squeezing off a parabellum round that struck the nearest camera's lens and dumped the whole contraption with a crash.

The actors were a heartbeat quicker on the uptake, bailing out of bed and lunging for their scattered clothes before they hit the exit running. Bolan let them go, as well as the second-unit cameraman who bolted on their heels. Four men remained, including the director, and while the warrior hoped to walk away without a body count, he had a message to convey.

"Two words," he told the bearded man. "Can you remember?"

"Sure." The guy appeared insulted, but he didn't feel like arguing.

"It's over. Tell Kenji, or whoever you've been dealing with. Make sure you get it straight."

"It's over."

"Beautiful. You get the part."

"That's all?"

"Unless you're wearing your asbestos jockstrap, I suggest you hit the bricks."

"I'm outa here!" the doorman said, immediately suiting words to action. He was followed closely by the others, as they left the Executioner alone.

He didn't hurry, but he didn't dawdle, either. Four thermite bombs emerged from the doctor's bag and were dispensed in swift succession. One lighted up the rumpled king-size bed, its white-hot embers scouring the room before he lobbed another down the hall and turned away. He dropped a third one in the spacious kitchen, saving number four to smoke the sunken living room, then made his way outside.

All things considered, Taoka could afford another house this size from petty cash, but real estate wasn't the issue. For the local ruler of the Yakuza, it was another loss of face to be redressed. Another explanation to the men at home.

And Bolan wasn't finished yet, by any means.

In fact the Executioner had barely hit his stride.

13

Sometimes, despite his basic faith in karma, Sam Jiangsu was still surprised when Fate stepped in to take a hand in the affairs of men. Today, he thought, was such a time.

It might have taken days for him to carry out the orders passed along by David Chan, except for Fate. He knew that Lisa Yau mistrusted him, despite his long association with her father, and he marveled at the fact that she could almost see through his disguise.

Almost.

With the conceit of youth, she still believed that he desired her body. There'd been a time, of course, when it was true, but she'd grown too old, and he'd never have approached his partner's child, in any case. Still, she was visibly uncomfortable in his presence, hesitant to speak, as if attracting his attention was the worst thing in the world. A little tramp like that, who doubtless spread her legs for all the round-eyed college boys.

Jiangsu had been mulling over ways and means of snaring Lisa, knowing in advance she'd refuse a meeting—or at least suspect his motives—when her call came through. Her voice was troubled as she spoke in guarded generalities about a nameless problem she couldn't resolve without his help.

Of course.

Without the microphone in Wong Yau's office, Sam Jiangsu wouldn't have understood. Forearmed with knowledge of the pit that Yau had excavated for himself, and Lisa's fear of risks inherent in a war against the Chu Lien Pang, he knew precisely what she wanted to discuss.

It was ironic, he decided, that her quest for the solution to a personal dilemma should resolve his own.

Poetic justice.

Jiangsu didn't permit himself to think about the fate that lay in store for Lisa after he delivered her to David Chan. It was enough for him to carry out the order he was given, as he had—in one form or another—from his days of childhood in Macao. Still young, he'd allowed himself to fantasize that Honolulu would be different, new and bright and clean. In some ways he'd been correct, but in the ways that mattered, nothing ever changed. His people were divided into predators and prey, with no rapprochement possible between the two.

Today a sacrifice of blood would rescue Sam Jiangsu from punishment, but the reprieve was only temporary. Soon, when Ho Lee had disposed of Yau and his other enemies, the hill chief of the Chu Lien Pang would ask another favor. And another.

No matter.

Such was life, and Jiangsu could never hope to change it. The best that he could hope to do was save himself, and so he'd performed his duty, phoning David Chan as soon as he arranged the rendezvous with Lisa. That which followed was inevitable, no responsibility of his.

Or so he tried to tell himself.

He wondered how it would be possible to face his friend and partner if Wong Yau discovered his involvement in the plan, but then he realized it wouldn't matter. By the time Yau learned the truth, if ever, it would be too late. Death silenced recriminations, and there was no vengeance from the grave.

Jiangsu checked his watch again—almost a minute since the last time—and determined to relax. Chan's soldiers would be waiting at the rendezvous, and he had to be in place before the girl arrived. The timing was essential for his own protection, and he dared not risk a deviation from the plan.

He knew that nothing would absolve him from the guilt he bore today. It was a shadow that would haunt him to his grave, but living with the guilt was preferable to death. Survival was the key to everything, a truth Wong Yau had managed to forget with age. A dead man's honor might inspire the poets, but it did the dead man no good whatsoever.

And Sam Jiangsu had chosen to survive, no matter what the cost.

IT BOTHERED Andrew Yau to go behind the old man's back, but he was sick and tired of sitting on the bench and waiting for a summons while the hottest action of his life unfolded on the streets. For years he'd been swallowing his pride and anger, watching as the Chu Lien Pang skimmed off a piece of every dollar that his father earned. It had been Andrew's future going down the tube, and Lisa's, but the old man silenced any arguments with reference to the risks involved with any move against the Triads.

Lately, though, his father had begun to change. It might be age, or simple recognition of the fact that he'd been a whipping boy too long, but either way, the shift was evident. It started with an occasional angry reference to the Triad scavengers, and escalated into war, his father forging an alliance with men from the mainland.

Andrew Yau wasn't a racist—or at least he didn't *think* he was—but life had taught him there were varying degrees of trust. Above all else he trusted in himself, with Lisa and their father tied for second place. His friends came next, and after them, his people as a whole. The white man, based on personal experience, would have to wind up somewhere near the bottom of the heap.

And yet the round-eyes had been kicking ass.

He didn't trust their motives necessarily, but if they really meant to help the family, Andrew thought that he should lend a hand. He'd be twenty-one next month, and he'd voted in the last election, even signed up for the non-existent draft. He was a man, and so it galled him doubly that his father viewed him as a child.

When it became apparent what was happening—the random strikes against Yakuza and Chu Lien Pang—he'd approached his father, pleading for an opportunity to serve. Though couched in terms of love, the ultimate rebuff was no less painful, wounding Andrew's ego as he understood the old man didn't trust him to perform.

It would be Andrew's job to demonstrate that he'd come of age.

The round-eyes would accept him when they saw what he could do, but he couldn't confront the Triads with his nerve alone. An equalizer was required, and Andrew had one waiting.

While his father disapproved of guns—or had, before his recent change of heart—a spate of robberies had prompted him to buy a pistol several years ago, to bolster the impression of security around the office. As it happened, YJ Enterprises—named for Wong Yau and his partner, Sam Jiangsu—was never robbed, and no one ever had to use the .38 that still resided in a filing cabinet drawer.

Until today.

A quick stop by the office, in and out before the secretary had a chance to question him, and Andrew Yau would be prepared to face his enemies. Undoubtedly the Chu Lien Pang had heavier artillery on hand, but he was counting on surprise to see him through. With any luck he might pick up a little something more substantial on the way.

The thought of shooting someone had intimidated him for a while. He still had qualms, an empty tingling in his stomach when he pictured all that noise and blood, but he knew that people killed one another every day, without contracting some disease or suffering a nervous breakdown in the process.

Gearing up for it was half the battle, and he'd accomplished that by dwelling on the times he saw his father livid with humiliation, standing silent while the Chu Lien Pang collectors helped themselves to cash or merchandise. These days the runners were a bunch of hoodlums in their teens, and still the old man was intimidated into paying for the pleasure of their company. It was enough to make him seethe, and Andrew thought that it would see him through.

The other half of killing, he decided, wasn't just the act itself, but everything that happened afterward. He was preparing to commit a crime, and while Hawaii had no death penalty, he didn't relish the idea of spending years in prison. He'd have to choose his target, think the action through before he made a move, but if he didn't put the wheels in motion now, he was afraid that fear might cancel his determination, stop him from delivering on the promise he'd made himself.

Approaching from the west, he pulled up at the intersection nearest to his father's office, waiting for the light to change. In front of him the year-old Buick owned by

Sam Jiangsu was emerging from the parking lot. It was a
break to have Sam taken care of, with his father back at
home. There'd be no one to question him or try to interfere.

But Andrew froze as Jiangsu picked up a tail, a sporty
compact falling into place behind him as he drove away. It
didn't take a genius to decide the occupants were Chu Lien
Pang, their shades and slicked-back hair announcing them
to anyone who knew the streets of Chinatown.

And they were after Sam!

There was no time to stop and fetch the pistol now. With
no clear means of knowing what the gunmen had in mind,
he instantly assumed the worst. The Triads were retaliat-
ing with a hit on Sam Jiangsu, but there was still a chance
to stop them, save his father's oldest friend, if he was quick
enough.

The light turned green, and Andrew became a part of
the parade, content to watch and wait until the gunners
made their move. He needed time to think, in any case,
and every second counted.

It wasn't what he had in mind, but the young man had
found his war.

And when the action broke, he'd be going in unarmed.

THE COFFEE SHOP had been selected as a kind of neutral
ground. The choice of meeting places had been left to Lisa
when she made it clear she wouldn't meet with Jiangsu at
her home or at his office. He'd countered by suggesting
several restaurants controlled by YJ Enterprises, but she
shied away from any meeting on her father's property.

It was enough that she had to go behind his back.

The call to Sam Jiangsu hadn't been easy. She could almost feel him staring at her through the telephone, and
while she knew the feeling was irrational, it lingered all the

same. Their business would be cut-and-dried, if Lisa had
her way, but she expected arguments against her personal
involvement in the struggle shaking Honolulu. He'd try to
talk her out of it because she was a woman and the
daughter of a friend, but he wouldn't succeed.

The tricky part, she knew, would be enlisting his cooperation. It would smack of treachery, a move against her
father, and she was prepared to bully him...or to play
upon what she believed were his affections, if it came to
that. It would have been obscene to lead him on directly,
but a smile was cheap enough, all things considered. If his
own mind made a friendly gesture more than what it was,
well, it wouldn't be Lisa's fault.

She waited in the car for Jiangsu, unwilling to proceed
until the older man arrived. With any luck they might
conclude their business in the parking lot. A name or address, anything at all, and Lisa could resume her search for
Mike Belasko with the odds against her ultimate success
reduced, however slightly.

Ten minutes sitting in the sun, and finally she saw
Jiangsu's car approaching, signaling the turn. He spotted
her and found an empty slot with three cars in between.
Emerging from her sports car, Lisa watched him lock the
Buick, putting on a smile she didn't feel in answer to his
own.

Diplomacy. It had a place within the family circle, as in
politics.

"I'm glad that you could get away," she said.

Small talk between conspirators, but what was wrong
with her father's partner? His face seemed frozen, more a
grimace than a smile, and he was staring past her shoulder in the direction of the street.

She turned in time to see a compact car pull in, its driver
pointing at her while his passenger prepared to disem-

bark. She didn't know the men by name, but there could be no doubt about their pedigree.

Their victims quickly learned to recognize the Chu Lien Pang on sight.

Lisa glanced again at Sam, his first expression of surprise replaced by something more like shame. Behind her she heard the others coming, then understanding in a flash that she'd been betrayed. Her father's oldest friend and business partner was surprised at being followed by members of the Triads, but he'd expected others to be waiting at the scene.

She bolted, glimpsing movement on her flank as two men raced to intercept her, joined immediately by the shotgun rider from the compact car. No shooting, yet, and Lisa wondered if they meant to stab her, or—

A hand reached out to snag her blouse in back, and Lisa wrenched away, the fabric ripping as she managed to avoid the lunge. Sidestepping, she didn't attempt to reach her car. The men would be on top of her before she had a chance to turn the key in the ignition, and she'd be dead an instant later. Safer on her feet, she looked for sanctuary in the coffee shop, where she could scream for help and barricade herself inside the rest room—anything to stall for time while the employees telephoned police.

A screech of tires from the direction of the street made Lisa hesitate, and in that moment she was lost. She caught a glimpse of her brother Andrew staring through the windshield of his car, before he rammed the idling compact from behind. She saw the driver lose his glasses, grimacing as he was slammed against the steering wheel, and then a flying tackle brought her down. Rough hands prevented her from lashing out, and others gripped her ankles, hoisting Lisa off the ground. She snapped and spit at them, like a cornered animal, but there was nothing she could do to free herself as she was borne away in the direction of a waiting Cadillac.

Suddenly there was a clap of thunder in her ears. She twisted in her captors' grip, the scream spontaneous as number three squeezed off another shotgun blast through Andrew's windshield.

Wriggling desperately she caught a mouthful of the nearest hardguy's sleeve and felt the muscle underneath. He bellowed in surprise and pain, releasing her, while his companion kept a firm grip on her legs. The end result was totally predictable, though Lisa's fear and rage had blurred her natural reception to the obvious. The drop was short—four feet, if that—but it was ample, as her skull struck pavement with the impact of a hammer stroke.

A blinding flash of pain, and she was lost in darkness, falling endlessly as gunfire echoed in her brain.

HE RECOGNIZED THE ANXIOUS tone when Tommy Anders picked up on the second ring.

"Hello?"

"I'm checking in," Bolan said.

"Jesus, I was getting worried. Have you heard?"

"I've been a little busy," Bolan answered. "Fill me in."

"It's hit the fan," the comic told him, sounding bitter. "Shooters put a move on Lisa Yau and brother Andrew. Damned near killed the kid. Nobody's seen or heard a thing from Lisa since the snatch."

The warrior's stomach twisted at the news.

"How long?"

"Half hour, give or take. The Bureau's on it, helping HPD, but all they've got is a description of the compact car a couple of the goons were driving. Andrew bashed it from behind before they started shooting at him. Chances are we'll find it burned out in a dump somewhere a couple weeks from now. I'll bet my pension it was hot to start with."

"Where's the boy?"

"They checked him into Queens for observation. Possible concussion from the crash, but otherwise he looks to be okay. Dumb luck they missed him with a scattergun at fifteen feet."

"Our luck, if he can tell us anything."

"Don't hold your breath. He talked to the police already, but it's pretty vague. He counted four, five guys—all Triads, by the sound—but then all hell broke loose, and they were blasting at him. No idea what happened to his sister, anything like that."

"I'd like to see him anyhow."

"No sweat. I'll meet you there in case the bluesuits try to stall."

"I'm on my way."

He cradled the receiver, moving swiftly to his car. In motion Bolan cursed himself for not anticipating this development or taking steps to guard against it. He'd been counting on his enemies to strike at one another as the heat increased, but Ho Yuan Lee had shifted his attention in a new direction. Snatching Lisa Yau might be a measure of retaliation, or one step toward the ultimate destruction of her father. Either way it spelled bad news for Bolan and his war.

Aside from the distraction and the risk to innocents, which he had dreaded going in, it meant there was a traitor in the friendly camp. Without a leak Ho Lee would still be blaming leaders of the Yakuza for his predicament, preparing for a gang war in the streets.

Someone had fingered Yau, his family, and all of them were now potentially at risk. Until he could identify the leak and plug it with a bullet, none of the civilians who had placed their trust in Tommy Anders would be safe.

The first step was a word with Andrew Yau. From there it would be anybody's guess.

Without a solid lead, he couldn't spare the time required for hunting traitors. Bolan would be forced to seek the girl instead, and spare no effort in a bid to set her free.

The war in Honolulu was about to escalate, from brushfire status to another plane, no quarter asked or given. He'd rattled his opponents from the start, but he'd have to crush them now. No other choice remained.

And if he failed to rescue Lisa Yau, God help the bastards who had kidnapped her.

14

Bolan caught the light at Vineyard Boulevard and turned right on Punchbowl, traveling two blocks before he wheeled his car into the visitor's parking lot of Queen's Hospital.

As he approached the reception desk, Tommy Anders flagged him from a corner of the waiting room. The warrior veered in that direction, catching up with Anders at the elevators.

"HPD has him in a private room, fourth floor. The doctors want him to stay overnight for observation, but he seems okay. It's got to be a miracle they didn't take his head off with that shotgun."

"Is he covered?" Bolan asked.

"A uniform, but he's expecting us. They like to keep it casual if they can."

"Suits me."

The elevator smelled of disinfectant, a pervasive odor that marked hospitals around the world. They disembarked on four and found the bluesuit idling at the nurses' station, chatting up a blonde. A sign from Anders put him back at ease, and he dismissed the comic's new companion with a passing glance.

"They call this tight security?"

"I told you it was casual. They figure Andrew blundered into something, and his sister was the target. If the

Mob was serious about the kid, they would've stuck around and done it right.''

"So, what's the rundown?"

"Four, five guys snatched Lisa Yau outside a coffee shop on Beretania. Kid was meeting her, he says, but traffic slowed him down. He got there just in time to see the bums move in. He rammed one car, then someone opened up with double-ought. Next time he had the nerve to raise his head, he's sitting there alone.''

"You buy it?" Bolan asked, as they approached the numbered door to Andrew Yau's room.

"I'd say it needs some work. No doubt about the ramming and the gunplay, but I'd swear he's keeping something to himself.''

"Such as?"

"No reading. Sorry.''

"Can I talk to him alone?"

"My pleasure.''

It was warm and bright inside the private room, with sunlight streaming through the blinds. The mindless racket of a game show emanated from a television mounted on the wall. If Andrew Yau was interested he didn't let it show, his eyes on Bolan as the Executioner approached his elevated bed.

"We need to talk.''

"I talked to the police already.''

"So I heard. I'd like to hear the rest of it.''

"What rest?"

"The part you didn't feel like sharing with the uniforms. You're covering. I need to know the who and why.''

"My sister's been kidnapped," Andrew said, his voice an angry rasp. "The bastard's tried to kill me. Why the hell would I be covering for them?"

"It never crossed my mind.''

"What, then?"

"Your father owns a chain of restaurants. Why meet your sister in a coffee shop on Beretania?"

Taken by surprise, the boy was silent for a double heartbeat, finally shrugging. "I don't know. It wasn't my idea."

"Whose was it?"

"That's a stupid question."

"Was there someone with your sister, Andrew?"

"Yeah. The pricks who grabbed her. Put them in a lineup and I'll introduce you."

"Someone else?"

"Like who?"

He waited, watching him sweat.

"I'll tell you what I told the cops," Yau said at last. "I got a call from Lisa. She had something that she didn't want to mention on the phone. She picked the coffee shop, but lunchtime traffic hung me up and I was late. A minute earlier, they might have grabbed me, too."

"The name?"

"*What* name?"

"The coffee shop."

Yau's cocky tone gave way to something very much like desperation. "Christ, I don't remember. Everything that's happened, how the hell can I remember that?"

"It was the last thing that your sister told you, right? And you were navigating on your own. You had to find it somehow."

"What? You're saying that I wasn't there because I can't recall the name?"

"Oh, you were there, all right. But something tells me you were playing tag."

"I don't know what—"

"Who were you following?"

The young man paled, but caught himself.

"You want to find somebody, try my sister. Bring her home why don't you?"

"That's the plan. It wouldn't hurt for you to share the information you've been keeping to yourself."

"You're crazy."

"Fine. We go the long route, then. I hope you've got the stones to live with your mistakes."

Outside, Anders wore a hopeful face until he got a look at Bolan's.

"Nothing?"

"You were right about the stonewall, but I don't have time to break him down."

"Okay, then what?"

"A different angle of attack."

"Aw, shit."

"If Hal's got any pull with HPD, he couldn't find a better time to use it. I'll need room to move without a lot of bluesuits getting in the way."

"I doubt they'll play along with what you have in mind."

"In that case maybe I can stay one step ahead and dazzle them with footwork."

Or a body count, he thought, emerging from the elevator, dropping Tommy Anders at a phone booth in the lobby, leaving him to make the necessary calls. If Washington could smooth the way, all right. If not, it made no difference to the Executioner.

He was about to gamble with the lady's life, and no official blessing would absolve him if he failed.

A HOUSEWIFE FROM PEORIA was jumping up and down in time to loud, discordant music, thrilled to death that she'd won a brand-new car. It didn't matter squat to Andrew

Yau, but he'd left the television on for background noise, in case the cop was parked outside his door.

The officer would never hear him dressing. Not unless he had another dizzy spell and tumbled on his ass.

He'd considered waiting for a while, perhaps until the sun went down, but Mike Belasko's visit and a nagging sense of urgency prevented him from stalling any longer. He didn't think the Triads meant to kill his sister right away—they could have done that in the parking lot with all the hardware they were packing—but he'd begun to picture Lisa in their hands, imagining the ways her captors might amuse themselves until the time was right.

What were they waiting for?

He didn't have to ponder long and hard on that one. Leverage was the answer, using Lisa as a weapon to attack their father. If the simple grief occasioned by her death was all the Chu Lien Pang desired, she'd have been gunned down outside the coffee shop. It must be something else—some kind of blackmail scheme, perhaps—and that gave Andrew hope that she was still alive. He might have a chance to set her free.

But first he had to free himself.

His head was pounding as he finished zipping up his slacks, and he sat on the bed to keep from falling as he went to work on socks and shoes. The doctors had suggested that he spend the night for observation, but the guard outside his door let the young man know that the suggestion was, in fact, an order. He hadn't been formally arrested, and the various detectives hadn't bothered reading him his rights, but he was still in custody. And he couldn't help Lisa from his bed, while game show bimbos yammered from the boob tube mounted on the wall.

He finished dressing, feeling like an idiot as he proceeded to the door. A glance should tell him whether he was trapped, or whether he had a chance. If he was spotted peeking out, the game was up.

The knob turned smoothly, soundlessly, as Andrew cracked the door to peer outside. No uniform immediately visible. He risked another inch, then edged his head outside, prepared to jerk it back at once if he was seen.

The cop was fifty feet away, distracted by some honey at the nurses' station. With his back turned, he couldn't see Andrew, and he had blocked the nurse's view, as well. The bad news was that Andrew couldn't reach the elevators from his room unless he passed within a few feet of the officer.

No good.

He took a chance and turned his head, examining the hallway to his right. The service stairs were twenty feet away, but he'd have to cross the corridor to reach them, taking care to make no noise and thereby give himself away.

He took a breath and held it, slipping from his room and waiting long enough to let the door ease shut behind him. Fine, so far. He crossed the hall with even, measured strides, refusing to look back and check the nurses' station. They'd either spot him or they wouldn't. Worrying about it was a waste of time.

Too late, he wondered what would happen if the access door was locked. It wasn't, and he stepped inside the stairwell, taking extra care to close the door without a sound. A giant number, painted on the wall directly opposite, informed him that his floor was number four.

Eight flights of twelve stairs each before he reached the ground. From there, unless they had a lookout on the street, he should be on his own.

Wheels, first, no matter what he had to do. On foot he was an easy target for police or members of the Chu Lien

Pang, and it would take all night for him to carry out his self-appointed duty.

After wheels, the office. He'd need the .38, now more than ever, and he had a key to let himself inside if it was after closing time when he arrived.

He'd grab the .38, and then pay a little visit to his "uncle," Sam Jiangsu.

He had some questions for the man who stood and watched while Lisa was abducted, then escaped before police arrived, the "friend" who kept his silence and avoided the police, refusing to provide descriptions of the criminals.

In retrospect Sam's silence came as a relief to Andrew. If the old man had spilled his guts to the detectives, the younger man would have lost his edge. There'd be nothing left to ask, no way of paying back Jiangsu's treachery.

This way, the old man would be his, and Jiangsu would answer all his questions, one by one.

Before he died.

No longer dizzy, Andrew Yau drew strength from his consuming anger as he started down the stairs.

EXPERIENCE TOLD BOLAN there was no point yet in grieving for Lisa Yau. The Triads wanted her alive, at least for now, and that gave Bolan time to make them reconsider their selected strategy. He hoped that Anders or Brognola would be able to arrange a truce with HPD, but once the fireworks started, it was anybody's game. The only winners were the ones who walked away.

And some of them would carry scars for life.

He launched the new, improved Hawaiian blitz on River Street, two blocks below the district's famous mall. The target was a nightclub frequented by prostitutes and managed by the Chu Lien Pang society, appealing to the servicemen and single tourists who were more concerned about companionship than cash. The joint wouldn't be open for a few more hours, but a cleaning crew was on the job, and Bolan used a service entrance at the back.

A bouncer moved to intercept him on the dance floor, but the sight of Bolan's Uzi made him reconsider. The warrior marched him back in the direction of a private office, picking up a bartender along the way. It was a squeeze, but he fit both of them inside a narrow pantry, halfway down the hall, and wedged a chair beneath the knob to keep them there.

He didn't bother to knock when he reached the office. One swift kick announced his presence, and he stepped across the threshold with his submachine gun leveled at the waist, prepared to answer any challengers.

A heavyset Chinese was seated on the far side of the desk, engaged in counting stacks of money. To his left and right, two sluggers of uncertain breed reacted with a speed that did them credit, even if it wasn't good enough to save their lives.

On Bolan's left, the taller of the pair was reaching underneath his flowered shirt to palm a handgun when a burst of parabellum manglers lifted him off his feet and hurled him backward. He rebounded off a filing cabinet, arms outflung as if to catch himself before his forehead smacked the desk with a resounding thud.

His partner wore an ankle holster to prevent his gun from showing through a fishnet muscle shirt, and he was hopping on his right foot, clutching at the upraised left, as Bolan swung around to bring him under fire.

"Aw, shit."

The Uzi chattered, stitching him across the chest and blowing him away before the shiny nickel-plated piece cleared leather. Going over backward in a rush, the guy touched down with force enough to drive his left knee against his chin.

It would have hurt like hell if he'd been alive.

The Chinese was watching Bolan, keeping both hands carefully in sight, a sheen of perspiration making him look freshly oiled.

"If you want the money, friend, it's yours."

"I'll take it," Bolan told him amiably, "and I'll give you something in return."

"What's that?"

"Your life, and some advice."

"Sounds good to me."

"Your boss just took delivery on a special package down on Beretania Street. It's not his property. He's risking everything he has to play a sucker bet. I want the package back, intact, or he can kiss it all goodbye. You got that?"

"Package. Beretania. Give it back or else."

"That's close enough."

"Is there a deadline on delivery?"

"I want it yesterday. Until I have the item safe in hand, I keep on kicking ass."

"So, how is anyone supposed to get in touch? I mean, in case they hear some news."

"I've got his private number. Have him standing by. After a few more stops I just might feel like chatting for a while."

"Okay. You got a name?"

A marksman's medal hit the desk between his hands.

"Pass that along. If it requires an explanation I can brief him when I call."

"The money?"

"Sack it up." He raised his Uzi as the man began to reach below his desk. "And think about how bad you want to live before I see those hands again."

"I hear you."

Moments later he was in the parking lot, heading toward his car. The message and the medal would be passed, he knew, but there was no predicting Ho Yuan Lee's reaction to the threat. If he didn't immediately recognize the Bolan calling card, a call or two would clear up the situation. And then what?

It was anybody's guess.

His opposition wouldn't fold at once, of that much he was certain. Lee might try to stall for time, negotiate, or he might launch his own offensive, using Lisa as a pawn. Whatever, it was Bolan's job to keep the heat on, make the enemy believe that any counterthrust would cost him dearly in the end.

The risk to Bolan's life was one thing, but he had to think of Lisa Yau, as well. A single error, and the game would go to his opponents by default. To win, he couldn't even let the bastards score.

And there was still the Yakuza to think about, when he could find the time to spare. Uncomfortable with the odds, he wondered briefly whether he had spread himself too thin this time.

He put the dark sedan in gear and headed for his next target.

Ho Yuan Lee would have his message by the time he struck again, but Bolan wanted two or three more hits behind him before he made the call. He needed credibility, and he'd have to purchase it with blood.

15

Marijuana is still the drug of preference in Hawaii, with sales earning growers and dealers an estimated three billion dollars each year, but the authorities are conscious of a rising trend toward the use of crystal methamphetamines. So popular is "speed" or "crank," that importation from the mainland will no longer meet demand, and meth labs have been spreading through the islands like a cancer, many of them planted on Oahu to be near their greatest source of revenue.

It doesn't take a genius to prepare a batch of speed. The basic components for crank are N-methyl formamide and phenyl acetone—a controlled substance produced in a simple four-step process, using legal materials available from most chemical supply stores. The base chemicals are cooked for six hours, give or take, to produce white, granular methamphetamine. The final product may be snorted or mixed with water and mainlined, affecting the human body much like an overdose of adrenaline. Users experience elevated blood pressure and decreased appetite for food, with insomnia often lapsing into methamphetamine psychosis. The end result is virtually indistinguishable from violent paranoid schizophrenia. Crank addicts rely on barbiturates, alcohol and opiates in order to "come down."

And occasionally they kill themselves.

The largest meth lab on Oahu was a native operation "licensed" by the Yakuza, concealed inside a house abutting Kapalama Stream, northwest of downtown Honolulu. After knocking over one of Ho Lee's smaller fan-tan parlors back in Chinatown, the Executioner selected his next target with a surgeon's skill.

He wasn't striking at the Chu Lien Pang directly, but the shock waves would be strong enough to shake loose something in the Triads.

It was all another way of making waves.

He wore a ski mask this time, with a pair of clip-on shades that would conceal his eyes without obscuring vision. There was nothing he could do about his size, but he was counting on the elements of fear, confusion and excitement to distort the memories of those who managed to survive.

He'd need at least one verified survivor for the plan to work. It wouldn't matter if the guy was wounded, but he'd have to be coherent, and he had to hang on long enough to pass the word.

Beyond that, he could fry in hell.

The lab was too expensive to be run without security— at least a team of guards—but Bolan had no time to scrutinize the layout and prepare elaborate strategy. He saw the Oriental gardener puttering around the flowerbeds outside a stylish country home, and he was ready when the little man reacted to his presence with a blur of motion, throwing down his shears and reaching for the stubby SMG he carried in his wheelbarrow.

The guy had obviously practiced, sharpening the move until he had it down, but practice and reality were two entirely different things. The fastest gun alive can do his thing in front of mirrors every time, but in a killing situation his reactions would be tempered by surprise, instinctive hesitation, fear.

Enough to get him killed.

The Asian's submachine gun had been fitted with a suppressor, not unlike the one attached to Bolan's Uzi. Both of them went off, the gardener's a trifle slower. The guy reeled, going over backward in the shrubbery before he got around to triggering a wild burst.

The warrior circled to the rear and found another gunner staking out the patio, preventing access to the kitchen door in back. The guy was either stoned or stupid, deafened by a Walkman when he should have been alert and listening for enemies. Reclining on a chaise longue with his ankles crossed, eyes nearly closed, he didn't hear the gardener's last stand and never had a chance to use the silenced Ingram SMG that lay across his lap.

No time for introductions, as the man in black dispatched a 3-round burst to close the lookout's concert with a bang. He hit the back door with a flying kick and crossed the threshold running, two more gunners gaping at him in the kitchen.

One of them, a slim Hawaiian seated at the kitchen table, made a move in the direction of his shoulder holster, cursing as he saw that it was hopeless. Half a dozen parabellum rounds ripped through his T-shirt, toppling his chair and body with a crash that seemed to shake the house.

So much for secrecy.

The chef was diving for a riot shotgun, propped beside a door that opened on the dining room, when Bolan stitched a burst along his spine. His body blocked the doorway, but it wasn't much of an obstruction. Bolan stepped across and let his nose direct him to the lab.

Four men, alerted by noises from the kitchen, looked up in confusion as the Executioner made his entrance, Uzi up and ready. The final gunner was a sawed-off runt who looked absurd in his ill-fitting muscle shirt and baggy pants, but he was handling his M-1 carbine like a pro. The first round was a freebie, passing inches to the left of Bolan's face, and then the Uzi answered with precision, cutting off the option of a second try. The gunner vaulted backward, landing on a table lined with laboratory glassware, and the fragile sculpture buried him.

That left the chemist and a flunky, decked out in pretentious lab coats, with an older Japanese whom Bolan took to be the man in charge. He wondered if the cooker and his pal were students, part-time lab technicians in a doctor's office or a hospital, and finally decided that it didn't matter. If they were involved they were dead.

The Asian managed not to scream, but Bolan saw the wet patch spreading on his slacks. So much for saving face.

"You want to die?"

"I'm not afraid," the man replied. His trousers and his tone betrayed him as a liar.

"Let's pretend you have a choice."

"I would prefer to live."

"Smart choice. I have a message for Taoka. Can you manage that?"

The small man nodded stiffly, trying to preserve some dignity despite his clammy slacks.

"Okay. The word is, Ho Yuan Lee dislikes the competition. He wants Honolulu for himself. The Yakuza can get lost. You got that?"

"Get lost?"

"Feel free to improvise."

"I'll convey the message."

"Do that," Bolan said. "If you screw it up, I may be forced to reconsider your reprieve."

He kept the overseer covered until the door swung shut behind him. Alone, he scattered his incendiary sticks around the lab and in the kitchen, bailing out before they sputtered into life and the assorted chemicals began to catch.

It might not fly, but he had paranoia on his side. Bolan knew that Taoka's troops would make substantial allies in his drive against the Chu Lien Pang. A touch of irony, assuming it worked out.

And if it didn't, he'd scrubbed a major meth lab, all the same.

But it was time to make some calls, the Triad chieftain first, then Tommy Anders, covering the bases in the final hours of his Honolulu war.

Whichever way it went, the action couldn't last much longer. Life or death, defeat or victory, tonight would see the campaign run its course.

As Bolan started cruising for a telephone, he wondered who among his friends and enemies would be alive to greet the dawn.

HO LEE WAS WAITING for the phone call as instructed. Seated in his high-backed swivel chair, eyes closed, a marksman's medal resting in the middle of his empty desk, a casual observer might have thought that he was sleeping, but the Triad chief's mind was working overtime. He knew the enemy at last, and with that knowledge came an urgent need to shift his strategy.

The Yakuza, it seemed, were innocent of the attacks on Chu Lien Pang investments, just as Triad soldiers had been blameless in the recent violence suffered by the Japanese. A stranger was among them, sowing seeds of bitterness and playing both ends off against the middle, striving to foment a war that might destroy them both.

A stranger with a name.

Mack Bolan.

It had taken two brief calls for Lee to understand the medal lying on his desk. In California one of his associates recalled the Executioner's appearance in Los Angeles some months earlier, when he'd scourged a group of Chu Lien Pang's Vietnamese competitors. New York was more informative, relating bits and pieces of the Bolan history, refreshing Ho Lee's memory on incidents that had occurred before he left Hong Kong and moved to Honolulu in the service of the syndicate.

Somehow his operation had attracted the attention of the Executioner, a man who had defied the mainland Mafia for years on end, annihilating hundreds of Sicilians, from their soldiers on the street to capos in their lavish fortresses.

A man whose reputation said that he couldn't be stopped.

Ho Lee was not impressed by reputations, having seen firsthand how fact and fantasy were often merged as time passed, until a man of simple luck and average skill became a knight in shining armor to the masses. How else could one explain the rise of Mao Tse-tung, or Lee himself? False modesty aside, it was entirely possible for cunning men to build their own exaggerated reputations, magnifying each triumph and diminishing their losses, rising over time—and sometimes overnight—to the exalted status of a superman.

He wouldn't underestimate the Executioner, by any means. His family was reeling from a string of rapid-fire assaults, and his faulty judgment of the situation had directed a retaliatory strike against Wong Yau. Too late, he recognized the error of his ways.

And now this Bolan wanted Lisa back.

Ho Lee had mulled over the implications without discovering an answer. A solution to the riddle was postponed until such time as he had dealt with Bolan and removed the threat that hovered over his surviving operations.

Soon.

The girl would be his answer, Lee decided, but he had to wait until Bolan called.

His private line was monitored around the clock by three associates who worked in shifts, eight hours at a stretch, to answer any calls and pass the privileged callers on to Lee. Perhaps a dozen people in the world possessed Lee's number, and he sometimes went for days without a call, but each one he received was vital to the conduct of his business. Whether it was placed from Hong Kong, Bangkok or Taiwan, New York, Los Angeles or San Francisco, each incoming call was handled with dispatch and full respect. A capo of the Mafia or chieftain of the Triads would expect no less.

Mack Bolan would receive the selfsame courtesy when he decided it was time to call.

As if in answer to his mental cue, the telephone's red light winked on. Ho Lee resisted an impulsive urge to lunge for the receiver, waiting with a fair display of patience for the duty man to do his job. A moment later, when the soft knock sounded on his office door, he was prepared, his thoughts and vocal cords completely in control.

"Hello?"

"I hope you got my message."

There was nothing in the voice to offer an impression of the caller's physical appearance, but he sensed an underlying strength and resignation.

"All of them, I think. You might have saved us both considerable time by calling me direct."

"I had some time to spare," the Executioner replied.

"And now?"

"It's simple. You have Lisa Yau. I want her back. If she's undamaged I'd be willing to accept a cease-fire. Otherwise..."

He left the threat unfinished, letting Lee fill in the gaps with his imagination.

"I admire your confidence. One man, against so many. What if you should lose?"

"We *all* lose," Bolan told him flatly. "You won't be around to see the celebration when they ship in your replacement from the Chu Lien Pang."

Lee thought about the possibility of wiretaps, or a tape recorder fixed at Bolan's end, but from the information he'd gathered, it wasn't the man's style.

"Perhaps," he said, "but you forget the girl."

"Is that your epitaph?"

A chill began to work its way down Ho Lee's spine, beginning at his nape. It took a major effort of the will to keep a tremor from his voice.

"You want the girl, I see no problem in releasing her. It was an error to suspect her family of involvement in our recent difficulty."

"If she's damaged—"

"I assure you, she is fit. Some bruises, possibly, occasioned by the nature of her invitation. She hasn't been harmed in any way while sampling my hospitality."

"I'll want a public handoff," Bolan said.

"Of course."

"The Punchbowl. Have her there at five o'clock. If anybody else is waiting for me, you can name your beneficiary."

"I understand. But, where..."

"I'll make the contact. Just be sure the drop team isn't late."

"I pride myself on punctuality."

"That's good to know. If your boys screw up, at least you won't be late to your own funeral."

The line went dead before he could reply, and Ho Lee felt the angry color rising in his face. He made a point of cradling the telephone receiver gently, reaching for the intercom and summoning the guard outside.

"Yes, sir?"

"Bring David Chan immediately."

"Sir."

In silence Ho Lee checked his watch. No more than ninety minutes, by the time he had an opportunity to speak with Chan, but they would make it work. He had no choice.

The Executioner would be on guard, but there were ways to snare the wisest fox.

A timely funeral, indeed.

But it wouldn't be Ho Yuan Lee's.

"WHAT'S THIS?" Tommy Anders asked as the heavy suitcase clanked at Bolan's feet.

"Some party favors," the warrior replied, moving toward a sofa on the far side of the apartment's living room and settling in. "I'll leave the distribution up to you. The way things look right now, I thought your people might appreciate some backup."

Anders left the suitcase where it was and took a seat across from Bolan.

"You look worn out," he said, concerned.

"Not yet. I've got a few more hands to play before I pack it in."

"The girl?"

"I've made arrangements for a pickup. Lee was happy to oblige."

"You trust him?"

"Who said that? I'm going in with both eyes open and a few tricks up my sleeve."

"You mentioned backup," Anders said. "I wouldn't mind—"

"Forget it. You're coordinating friendlies on the other end. They'll need you if it blows up in my face."

"I hate this plan already."

"It's the best deal I could make. If Lee plays straight I'll back off far enough to let Taoka have his shot. If you and Hal can't bring it home from there we'll have to think again."

"And if he isn't playing straight?"

"Take that one as it comes. I made the man a promise, and I'll keep it if I can."

"I don't mind telling you that Wong Yau's pissed off. It's all that I could do to keep the guy from rounding up some boys and going after Lee himself. The crowd from Little Tokyo is getting action fever, too, from what I hear."

"Don't give them any room to run until we see what happens with the pickup. If it falls apart and you decide to field a team, make sure it's not old men and little boys."

"I'll do my best." The comic showed a flash of irritation, tempered by concern. "Of course if you want to see the job done right, you ought to stick around."

"I hadn't planned on going anywhere," the Executioner replied, still knowing it could happen. *Anything* could happen once he showed himself to Ho Lee's troops, and strategy would only count for half the battle, then.

The rest of it would be audacity and nerve, when everything he had was riding on the line. A dash of instinct, to complete the recipe, and Bolan would be winging it, against the odds.

But if he missed the lady...

Bolan blocked the pictures from his mind, refusing to consider the alternatives. Familiar forms and faces, frozen in the final moments of their lives, each counting on the Executioner to save them in a situation that had proved to be impossible.

Enough.

He couldn't raise the dead or turn the clock back, but he could make use of every waking moment he had left. For Lisa Yau and all the countless other victims yet unknown.

The Executioner could give it everything he had.

In fact it was the only way he knew to play the game.

16

Andrew Yau knew that Sam Jiangsu would not be in his office, but it never hurt to check. The .38 was in its usual place, and Andrew tucked it in his waistband underneath the lightweight sport coat that he wore. The secretary, winding down her day, didn't appear to notice, though she'd regarded Andrew with concern when he arrived.

"I thought that you—"

"They let me out ahead of time."

"Oh, well, that's nice."

She didn't know what else to say, and he was grateful for the silence as he finished with his furtive business, moving toward the door.

"I hope you're feeling better."

Turning on the threshold, Andrew forced a smile and said, "I will be, soon."

The Subaru with keys in the ignition had been a stroke of luck. He'd been pondering the transportation problem, painfully aware that he had no idea about the proper method of hot-wiring a car, when the answer presented itself. By now, he knew the owner would have missed it, telephoning the police, but auto thefts were as common as leis on Oahu. The odds of Andrew being spotted on the short drive that remained were slim, and he had no choice, either way.

Sam Jiangsu lived close to Chinatown, a side street off
Pauahi, like he couldn't stand to tear himself away. At least
he made it easy.

Andrew parked the vehicle a block away—no point in
giving nosy cops a starting point if they should happen on
the car by accident—and doubled back to reach the target
address. As he waited on the welcome mat for Jiangsu to
answer, Andrew felt anger welling up inside him.

It would be so easy, just a simple point and squeeze before the door was fully opened. One shot, maybe two, and
he'd probably be safe inside the car before the neighbors
understood that anything was happening.

An easy kill.

But Andrew needed information to help his sister and
avenge himself against the enemies who pulled Jiangsu's
strings.

He heard the dead bolt, braced himself and slipped one
hand inside his jacket as the door swung open. Sam
Jiangsu was startled, speechless, but it didn't matter with
the .38 pressed tight against his chest.

"Back up."

The man did as he was told, and Andrew closed the door
behind him, latching it. He scanned the empty living room
beyond and wagged his snubby pistol toward the couch.

"Sit down."

"Are you all right?" It was the first time Jiangsu had
spoken, and he sounded strange, as if he didn't know quite
how to handle chatting with a ghost.

"I'm fine," Andrew replied, settling in an easy chair
across the coffee table, facing Jiangsu. "You ought to
think about yourself."

The old man tried a bluff. "I don't know what you
mean."

"I saw you, *Uncle*. Did you think that I was blind? Or maybe you were hoping I would concentrate on Lisa being kidnapped, while you slipped away."

Jiangsu's eyes were moist as he replied. "You weren't supposed to be there, Andrew."

"Tell me something new. Where's Lisa?"

"Gone."

He cocked the .38, his finger on the trigger, weapon braced against his knee. "I don't have time for games," he snapped. "Straight answers just might save your life."

The old man tried to stare him down. "She's been taken by the Chu Lien Pang," he said. "What more is there to say? They don't inform me of their plans."

"But you keep *them* informed, is that the story?"

"Yes."

"How long?"

"It doesn't matter. There's nothing you can say that I haven't already told myself."

He gestured with the .38 and said, "It wasn't talking that I had in mind."

"Before you came, I planned to kill myself."

"You should have gone ahead."

"But I decided that I want to live."

"Bad choice, unless you've got some information you can trade."

"One thing..."

The move was quick enough that Andrew barely registered his danger, squeezing off without a chance to aim as Jiangsu lunged forward, thrusting one hand underneath the open magazine. His bullet drilled the wall, a perfect miss, and then the old man had a pistol in his hand, the muzzle looking like an open manhole.

The second time, they fired together, kept on firing as they twisted, writhing, sliding to the floor. Some rounds went wild, but others found their mark. Enough to do the job. On both men.

AT LEAST TWO HOURS remained before the sun went down, but Bolan didn't mind the daylight. He'd picked the hour and the place to give himself some combat stretch, a chance to spot his enemies if Ho Lee tried to spring a trap. And room to run, if necessary. The Punchbowl, a national cemetery, fulfilled his needs.

The warrior made another rapid scan and counted twenty-seven male adults and thirteen women. All of them couldn't be gunners, but their distribution through the cemetery meant that he could never hope to get a close-up look at each and every one before his time ran out. No way to check for bulges that betrayed a hidden gun beneath a shirt or suit coat, nothing he could do to neutralize the dark potential of a dozen handbags.

Resigned, he settled down to wait.

They showed up right on time—two Chinese men in business suits with a woman wedged between them like she couldn't find her way alone. The men wore shades, and they were definitely packing, but it wouldn't matter, if they followed his instructions to the letter.

If.

He let them clear the upper gallery and start downstairs, pretending they'd come to visit martyred friends or relatives. They fit the scene just fine, a little overdressed for the majority of browsers, but the time of day would readily explain that they'd come directly from work. Bolan recognized the outfit Lisa had been wearing at the teahouse and outside Trans-Global Modeling. The woman clutched her purse two-handed at her waist, as if to keep her hands from trembling visibly.

He didn't recognize the sunglasses, but what of it? Ho Lee had mentioned bruises, and he figured Lisa for a scrapper. If they had to deck her in the act of carting her away, he'd have bet that someone else was nursing bruises of his own.

When they'd traveled far enough for him to see they had no tail, the warrior started moving on an intercepting course. The acting wasn't critical, but Bolan hoped to keep it simple. Just a meeting on the stairs, and Lisa walked away on Bolan's arm, while her attentive escorts lingered for a while among the dead.

Like clockwork, right.

With twenty yards to go, he recognized the suck. The girl would pass for Lisa at a distance, but her choice had evidently been a hasty one, determined by her clothing size and the belief that white men think all Chinese look alike. To Bolan, with his years of personal experience in Asia, ringing this one in for Lisa Yau was tantamount to having Eddie Murphy try to pass as Sidney Poitier.

No go.

The shooters saw him coming, and all three reacted instantly. The two men dug for hardware while the woman dipped a hand inside her bag, withdrawing a shiny automatic. The bookends both wore stubby automatic weapons in convenient shoulder rigs, and they were spraying lead in unison as Bolan went to ground.

The headstones saved him, solid granite flattening a number of the slugs, deflecting others into whining ricochets. He palmed the Beretta and was bracing to return fire, when the bullets started coming in from Bolan's flank, as well.

He scrunched around in that direction, searching for his enemies. A squat Hawaiian with an automatic pistol sprinted toward the action, firing on the run. Behind the new arrival, still too far away to join the fight, two more Hawaiians and a haole gunner were unlimbering their hardware.

Ho Lee had covered all the bases. If his shooters didn't bag their man it wouldn't be for lack of trying.

Bolan took the short Hawaiian first, because the angle left them both exposed and he couldn't afford to bolt from cover. He triggered three quick rounds and saw the runner stumble, lurching with the impact of a parabellum round between his ribs. A second wound was spouting crimson from his throat.

One down and six to go, unless the Chu Lien Pang had other guns around the Punchbowl, waiting to assist if members of the first team dropped the ball.

Around him, up and down the gallery of graves, the real-life tourists were quitting the area, women screaming, men too busy running for their lives. The gunners didn't seem to care, and the Executioner had to figure they were under orders from the top. Take Bolan out, or don't come back alive.

It figured that a few of the tourists, at least, would telephone police, and Bolan knew the clock was running. In the long view it would be as bad for HPD to trap him here, as for the Triad shooters to complete their mission. Either way, he'd be dead, the difference of a day or two completely insignificant.

There would be two, three minutes, tops, before the first patrol cars started to arrive. If Bolan couldn't liquidate his opposition in the time allowed, he had to find a way around them, get access to the parking lot, his wheels, the highway.

The warrior risked a glance around the nearest headstone, dodging back immediately as the woman and a single SMG cut loose with concentrated fire. Their partner was reloading, and Bolan knew that it was now or never. He'd have to make his move before the others, closing from behind him, got close enough to pin him down.

They'd be looking for him in the far side of the headstone, counting on a savvy soldier to reverse directions and confound his enemy. Instead he rolled back toward the same side they'd sprayed brief seconds earlier—the right—and opened up with 3-round bursts at something close to fifteen yards.

The starboard shooter had his brand-new magazine in place, but he'd never have a chance to use it, as the parabellum shockers ripped across his chest from right to left. The impact spun him through a loose-limbed pirouette, his submachine gun spinning out of frame as lifeless fingers lost their grip.

Tracking, as the woman bolted, Bolan's mind closed to her sex as he unleashed another burst. She was a pro, and her intent made all the difference in the world. Two rounds ripped through her back, the third going wide before she had an opportunity to look for cover. Pitching forward on her face, the lethal lady gave a final tremor and lay still.

Her partner was returning Bolan's fire by that time, but his aim was high. He tried to sidestep, dodging, but he stumbled on a headstone and went down. The parabellum burst that should have knocked him sprawling missed completely, and the guy's own stream of fire was twisted, veering toward the clouds.

Another burst to pin him down, and Bolan saw him shudder as the three 9 mm rounds struck home. His dying finger clenched around the submachine gun's trigger, emptying the magazine without effect before the weapon dropped across his chest.

It would be now or never, Bolan realized. He burst from cover, glancing back in time to see the two Hawaiians and their haole backup sprinting for position. The warrior flicked the 93-R's fire-selector switch and gave them one round each without a break in stride. He didn't have a hope in hell of scoring, but the fire would slow them down, and Bolan needed every break that he could manufacture in what seemed to be a dead-end situation.

Charging up the stairs, he ditched the pistol's empty magazine and snapped another into place. Behind him someone tried a ragged burst of automatic fire, and Bolan heard the wet, distinctive sound of bullets slapping earth. He reached the exit, dodging past a couple who had gone to ground beneath a mural illustrating island warfare from another generation, ducking through the exit as another burst of hostile fire let go.

Another miss.

The Executioner reached his car. Once more he'd dispensed with the explosive charges, and it saved him time now as he slid behind the wheel. His opposition would have cars, as well, but they'd signed on for a simple hit-and-run inside the cemetery, and a running fight through downtown Honolulu would be something else again. He had a hunch that they'd let it go if Bolan got a decent lead and left them in his dust.

His hunch was right.

The shooters fired a concentrated volley at his taillights, breaking for their wheels as they discovered he was out of range. But after several blocks he saw no shadows, nothing to suggest pursuit. He took evasive measures, just in case, but after ten more minutes, Bolan knew that there was no mistake.

The hit team had decided not to overstep the bounds of their assignment, multiplying risks without the promise of significant reward. The slaughter had been business, after all, and nothing personal.

Except to Bolan.

He'd gambled on the Chu Lien Pang's commander to be sensible, aware the odds were fifty-fifty at the very best. Ho Lee had opted for a suck, and Bolan had reversed the play. They understood each other now.

But he'd made a promise to the Triad leader, regarding Lisa Yau. Ho Lee had shunned the bargain, and there was a price attached to his defiance.

If the Executioner had anything to say about it Lee was scheduled for a crash course in survival economics. It was strictly pass or fail, no graduation ceremonies, and the flunkies had no option to repeat the course.

They wouldn't live that long.

SACHIRO MATSUMOTO was delighted with his orders, and he took no pains to hide the fact. He'd grown tired of sitting on his hands and waiting for instructions while the Chu Lien Pang barbarians dismantled everything the Yakuza had worked for during recent months. Retaliation should have been approved at once, but it wasn't his place to second-guess his *oyabun* on such strategic matters.

Now at last the wise old men in Tokyo had put their heads together and decided on a course of action. He hoped it wouldn't be too late.

The Lincoln was a spacious vehicle with room enough for half a dozen men besides himself, and with the arms they carried, they could deal with a contingent several times their size.

And, for insurance, he had another eight men in the car behind him.

In essence he'd been unleashed to strike against the Chinese at will, and Matsumoto had compiled a list of targets that deserved attention. He'd save the best for last, and give Ho Lee a taste of things to come before he took the old man out. The last act was an honor Matsumoto was reserving for himself.

But first was the combination bank and lending office on North King Street, where the Triads doled out cash to needy fellow countrymen, exacting interest at the rate of twenty-eight percent per week. Matsumoto had no quarrel with the system—one the Yakuza at home had used with fine results for years—but he begrudged the Triads their success in Honolulu. Every dime collected from the peasants went to Ho Lee's war chest, and the first step in defeating any hostile army was disruption of their critical supplies.

Without the ready flow of cash, Lee's surplus stock of mercenary gunmen would evaporate. The dedicated members of his brotherhood would linger on, but even they were motivated by a basic greed, as much as any loyalty to the Chu Lien Pang society itself. When they began to die for nothing, Matsumoto thought that some of them might undergo a change of heart.

If not, they'd be executed all the same.

His driver parked across the street, the second Lincoln close behind them. Matsumoto issued his instructions via walkie-talkie, speaking in his native Japanese. It mattered not at all if some child's toy somewhere was tuned in to their frequency. The source of his transmission would remain a mystery, and by the time police knew what was happening, his soldiers would be gone.

In search of other targets, punishing Ho Lee.

They went in shooting, sparing no one, from the young receptionist out front to the incompetents with pistols in their armpits who attempted to defend the bank. Five bodies littered the floor in under sixty seconds, and Matsumoto knew that Kenji would be pleased. Efficiency was something to be proud of.

He didn't attempt to steal the cash piled up in cardboard boxes, stacked on folding tables and lined up against one wall. To steal from a defeated enemy would cost him face, while scorning the reward—or burning it—would be a worthy gesture of contempt against Ho Lee.

Matsumoto waited with the body of his troops, while two men doubled back to fetch the cans of gasoline. He watched them slosh the contents over furniture, the floor and crates of greenbacks, taking time to lay a trail between the counting room and exit. Matsumoto struck the match himself, remaining on the threshold long enough to see the flames take hold.

A job well done, but he was far from finished. Ho Yuan Lee had stirred a hornet's nest when he conspired against the Yakuza, and nothing would protect him from the stinging retribution he deserved.

Before the night was over, Lee would witness the destruction of his Honolulu empire. He wouldn't possess the honor or resolve to kill himself, and Matsumoto would be forced to help him.

Smiling, the Japanese thought it just might make his day.

17

Six mini-uzis lined the table, fitted with suppressors, loaded magazines in place. Spare clips were stacked between them, ammunition boxes laid out on the side. It made a lethal show-and-tell display, and the assembled guests were silent as they checked out the hardware, their nervous eyes returning frequently to Tommy Anders, who was seated on the couch.

Wong Yau had brought a bodyguard this time. He had no children left to stand beside him, but a young associate had tagged along to hear what Anders had to say. The young man didn't give his name, and Anders didn't ask.

Tsuyoshi Ino and his confidante, Toshiro, each brought younger bodyguards, as well. The comic didn't question their selection, trusting them to judge their own companions. Wong Yau's recent lesson might inspire some paranoia, but it wouldn't hurt to keep the others on their toes.

All things considered, Anders was surprised the Chinese businessman had kept his date at all. His son was lying on a slab downtown beside the ventilated body of an old and trusted friend.

So much for friendship.

But the older man was bearing up, a kind of granite resolution in his eyes and in his attitude, as if it would take more than treachery, the murder of his son and the abduction of his daughter to defeat him. And he studied the assembled Uzis with a fascination that gave Tommy Anders pause.

"These weapons have been borrowed, shall we say, from one of your antagonists. They're illegal as hell, but we thought, with the way things are going, you might be in the market for some self-defense."

"The Chu Lien Pang have weapons such as these," Wong said. "It doesn't make us even, but it's a start."

"Hold on." Anders raised a hand. "I'm not recruiting vigilantes here, okay? Belasko is the best we've got, and he's already on your daughter's case. When I said self-defense just now, that's what I meant. We don't need any more folks out there shooting up the streets."

As Anders spoke, he thought of Bolan's curt instructions. If it came to armed resistance—hell, if Striker failed—he was supposed to look for soldiers, not old men or boys who didn't know which way to hold the razor when they shaved. Of course the bodyguards might qualify, and there were probably some more like them at home.

But how could he refuse Wong Yau, whose family had been destroyed within the span of several hours? How could he deny Tsuyoshi Ino and the others after all that they'd suffered through the years? That kind of brooding anger would inevitably find a voice, if not with his and Bolan's help, then on its own. He felt the tension in his guests, a palpable sensation like the trembling of a glass before it shatters under ultrasonic waves. Anders understood that there was no way he could warn them off.

They'd already seen the worst their enemies could do, and they'd turned their backs on fear. Define it any way you liked—a hunger for revenge, or maybe just a quest for self-respect—but there was nothing Anders could have said or done to stem the rising tide. It was enough, perhaps, if he could slow them down and make damned sure they thought their moves out in advance.

"The way it stands," he said, "you've got a three-way hassle. We've been rattling the Triads and the Yakuza, to shake them up and keep them guessing, but the syndicates are also gearing up to take each other out. From late reports, the Yakuza has made a couple moves already, tightening their noose around the Chu Lien Pang. On top of that, the boys from HPD are cracking down the best they can."

"And Lisa?" There was deep anxiety in Wong Yau's tone.

"Belasko's working on it, like I said. We think she's still alive, but getting to her will require some fancy footwork. I'm afraid that anything your people try right now could jeopardize her safety. Maybe get her killed."

"My son is dead," Wong Yau replied. "I learn too late that my most trusted friend has been seduced into the service of my enemies. My loss begins and ends with trusting others."

On the far side of the table, Ino cleared his throat. "Wong-san speaks the truth. We, too, have reason to believe that some of our associates do more than pay their weekly tribute to the Yakuza. The enemy has eyes within our offices and homes. Their actions violate no law, but they must still be punished."

Anders frowned.

"Officially," he said, "I can't advise you to resist. You may be killed, and if you aren't, there's still a risk of winding up in jail. Possession of an automatic weapon means five years without probation in Hawaii, and you get the same for silencers. Beyond that, you'll be looking at a whole new list of felonies if anybody fires the goddamned things."

"I'm in prison now," the Chinese businessman responded. "I've lost my children to the Triads, and my oldest friend. If I don't stand up I'll be paying tribute to the Chu Lien Pang until they finally decide to kill me, too."

"I don't believe they'll get the chance. Belasko—"

"*I* don't believe in trusting others with my life. No more. The trust I placed in Sam Jiangsu has been rewarded with a dagger in the heart. Your friend means well, but he is one man, standing on his own against two armies."

Anders longed to tell them that it wouldn't be the first time, but his mandate didn't cover using Bolan's name. If Bolan dropped a marksman's medal here and there to rattle members of the opposition, it would be his choice. Meanwhile his fragile links with Washington were strictly off the record, and if someone blew the whistle, it wouldn't be Tommy Anders.

But he *could* provide some free advice to citizens who had their minds made up. Oh, yes.

"So, everyone's agreed?"

A round of cautious glances was followed by determined nods.

"Okay," he said, "I guess we'd better make some plans."

THE PUNCHBOWL SCAM demanded swift retaliation, and the Executioner had picked his target before the sounds of automatic fire stopped ringing in his ears. He wasn't ready for a move on Ho Yuan Lee directly—that would have to wait until dark, for Lisa's sake—but he could send a message to the Triad chief.

The mark was David Chan, Lee's number two and the recipient of one free warning, Bolan-style. The second time around, he didn't feel inclined to be so generous.

Chan's office was a ninth-floor suite that faced Pauahi Avenue, across the street from older buildings that didn't compare in height or glamour. All of them would go, in time, replaced by monoliths of glass and steel, but they were standing at the moment.

It was all the Executioner could ask.

He stopped outside a busy supermarket, rummaging inside the trunk of his sedan like any bachelor stowing groceries. In a minute flat he had the Marlin broken down and packed inside a metal toolbox. Slipping off his shoes and jacket, Bolan stepped into a faded jumpsuit with a zipper up the front. The cut was loose enough to cover his Beretta, and the name tag labeled him as "Mel." Without a close inspection, Bolan thought that his performance as a janitor would do.

It only had to get him on the roof.

His target, scouted in the predawn hours before the Honolulu blitz began, was a Pauahi high rise dating from the 1950s, occupied by lawyers, CPAs and a collection agency. Ten stories overall, it was a dwarf compared to the imposing office blocks across the street, but it would serve his purpose as a sniper's nest.

He parked in back and used the service entrance, waiting for the elevator with a couple of insurance salesmen talking business. Both of them got off on six, and Bolan rode it to the top. From ten he took a narrow, musty flight of stairs that led him to the roof, then crossed to face the other buildings on Pauahi Avenue, directly opposite.

A moment for the Marlin's reassembly, and he used the scope to fix his target, staying well back from the parapet to rule out any accidental sightings by pedestrians below. Chan's office was a floor beneath his vantage point, the inner sanctum magnified behind its wall of tinted glass. He saw the desk and high-backed swivel chair, the plush settee and coffee table for informal meetings, with a wet bar on the side.

At first he was afraid he might have missed the Triad's number-two man, but then a door swung open on the left, and David Chan emerged, still tucking in his tailored shirt.

The washroom. Fair enough.

He watched Chan cross the room and take his place behind the desk, already reaching for the telephone. Discussing strategy with Ho Yuan Lee, perhaps? Or handing down new orders to his soldiers on the street?

It made no difference, now. The Chu Lien Pang lieutenant's time was running out.

The windows were a problem, but the Marlin's handloads featured boattail projectiles with full-metal jackets, designed for maximum penetration with minimum deflection and deformity. They'd be traveling 2,000 feet per second when they struck the heavy, tinted glass, and while he wouldn't count on number one to score a kill, a rapid second round should pin Chan down before he had a chance to bolt.

Bolan lined the cross hairs up behind Chan's ear, allowing for a half-inch rise above the line of sight at forty yards. The marksman filled his lungs, released a portion of the breath and held the rest, his index finger curling slowly, evenly around the Marlin's trigger.

The recoil slammed against his shoulder like a solid punch, but it was nothing in comparison to what the bullet did downrange. Chan's window seemed to ripple, like a piece of cellophane, and then a plate-size chunk of it disintegrated, spraying jagged shards of glass across the room.

Bolan worked the lever action smoothly, holding target acquisition as the Chu Lien Pang lieutenant tried to swivel in his chair, reacting with the memory of one who had been under fire before.

Too late.

The Marlin's second round caught David Chan directly on the angle of his jaw, collapsing flesh and bone, the impact powerful enough to lift him from his chair and stretch him out across the desk.

It was time to make another phone call, just to let the Triad chieftain know his nemesis was still alive and well. Unlike the heir apparent to his throne.

It never hurt to kick a cannibal when he was down. Especially if it prevented him from getting up again.

Ho LEE WAS SICK TO DEATH of telephones. If possible he'd have had them all ripped out and thrown away to silence their incessant shrilling and allow his nerves to rest. Since the disaster at the Punchbowl—four of his best soldiers dead, the Executioner escaped without a scratch—the news had gone from bad to worse.

No sooner had he fixed on Bolan as his major enemy than he was set upon by gunners from the Yakuza. There could be no mistake this time, as witnesses reported better than a dozen Japanese involved in the destruction of his most productive loan shark operation. Five more were dead, and there were questions from police that he wasn't prepared to answer.

Now a call had reported that a madman with a rifle had assassinated David Chan, a young man Lee had groomed and educated, treated as the son he never had. Chan was the second most respected member of the Chu Lien Pang society outside of Hong Kong proper.

Of course the guards assigned to guard Chan with their lives had been in no position to protect him from a sniper, who'd been perched across the street. They *should* have been, considering the first attack on David's home that morning, but their preparations had been lacking. Someone would be punished, and severely, when he found the time.

Assuming, always, that he still had anyone to punish.

Fatalism was a part of Ho Lee's nature, but acceptance of the setbacks in his life didn't make him a pessimist. If anything he was accustomed to success, and now he wondered if the past few years had softened him, depriving him of the instinctive ruthlessness that placed him where he was today.

Impossible.

An aging tiger didn't lose its taste for fresh, raw meat. The cobra, hatched possessing venom strong enough to kill a man, was no less potent on the last day of its life.

Ho Lee hadn't forgotten how to fight, but he wasn't immortal, either. If he didn't swiftly take command of the events in Honolulu, he might well be pushed aside by younger men.

It was the crowning insult, and he refused to contemplate the possibility.

Lee would survive—and win—because he had to.

And, again, the telephone. His private line.

The houseman knocked, and Lee took pains to mask his irritation as he took the call.

"Hello?"

"You should have played it smart."

The grim voice set his teeth on edge. Lee was embarrassed by the chill that raced along his spine.

"I was obliged to test you," he replied. "A wise man only deals with worthy enemies."

"I know the feeling," Bolan said. "I had to give your buddy Chan a little quiz myself. Seems like he didn't do his homework."

Sudden tightness gripped Lee's throat. He swallowed hard and said, "He had no part in my decision. You have made a grave mistake."

"Too bad. I guess that means I owe you one. Expect delivery sometime soon."

Before he caught himself, Lee glanced in the direction of his flower garden, where a team of sentries stood on guard. No danger there.

Not yet.

"The girl no longer interests you?"

"*You* interest me," Bolan said. "With all this testing going on it's only fair to warn you. If you're smart you should be cramming for your finals."

"More threats?"

"A promise. You're on borrowed time."

The line went dead before he could respond, and this time Lee allowed himself to slam the handset down. It was a minor gesture of defiance, but it helped.

One man.

He'd done much to harm the family, but it was coming to an end. The round-eye's arrogance would press him into taking risks beyond his ultimate control, and he'd be destroyed, as were all who opposed the Chu Lien Pang.

It was inevitable. He couldn't escape.

Ho Lee would simply have to watch his back and take the necessary steps to guarantee survival while the madman was at large. Perhaps, if fortune smiled, the devil could be laid to rest that very night.

His death would be a cause for celebration, and the hill chief of the Chu Lien Pang already had a party favor waiting for himself.

He felt like smiling at the thought of Lisa Yau, but managed to suppress the urge. There was no time for levity while Bolan lived.

A few more hours, and he could afford to smile.

The hill chief put on his war face and reached out for the hated telephone.

"YOU HAD TO BE THERE," Tommy Anders said. "I tried to talk them out of it, so help me, but they had their minds made up. At least they've got some younger guys, for all the good that it'll do. A couple of them looked like vets."

Bone weary, Bolan stood inside a claustrophobic phone booth, his back turned toward the setting sun.

"They took delivery on the hardware?"

"Ate it up," the comic told him. "For the record, I advised them of the penalties and all, but they were on a roll. You want a briefing on the blood and honor theme, I've had it from the horse's mouth."

"Their call. God knows, they've been paying dues."

"No argument. I thought the deal with Andrew Yau would knock his father out, but he keeps coming back for more. The others, too."

"I won't have time to cover them," he said.

"I'm working on it. Nothing fancy, but I've learned a move or two along the way."

"Just watch yourself."

"Believe it, guy. You hear about the raid on Ho Lee's loan shark operation?"

"No. It wasn't one of mine."

"You might take credit for it, though. Seems like Taoka's had enough of sitting on his hands. His men are out there kicking ass and taking names."

"It couldn't hurt."

"So, what about the lady?"

"If she still has any chance at all, I have to make it for her," Bolan said. "I'm dropping by to pay a call on Lee tonight, once it gets dark."

"Need company?"

The prospect made him scowl. "That's negative. If you can steer your troops away from Lee's HQ, I'd be obliged."

"My troops? Don't kid yourself. The fact is, I've been trying to persuade them they should tackle something more their size."

"They buy it?"

"Far as I can tell. Whatever, I'm supposed to ride along—as an observer, natch—so I can try to head them off if things get sticky."

Bolan didn't envy Anders his task, but someone had to try to keep the amateurs in line. Without assistance they'd certainly be massacred.

"Good luck, or is it 'break a leg'?"

"Whatever, I can use it." From the sound of Anders's voice, he wasn't relishing the night ahead. "When we sit down on the other side of this, I need to think about the limits on my job description."

"Right. Why don't you pull the other one?"

"You think I *like* this shit?"

"You're not required to like it," Bolan told him.

"Just perform, I know. You sound like Hal."

"No time for flattery. I've still got calls to make before the main event."

"You should try working for a living."

"Yeah, I love you, too."

He severed the connection, moving toward his car. Another hour yet until the darkness settled on Oahu. He still had time to shake up Ho Lee's a bit, perhaps distract the troops and thin them out before he faced the dragon in his lair.

Preliminaries.

But his mind was working on the title bout, weighing odds and angles of attack. He had one chance to do it right, and if he blew it, Lisa Yau would be among the grim statistics tabulated by official mop-up teams.

One slip on his part and the lady wouldn't be alone.

18

Ho Lee's estate was north of town, off Round Top Drive. Unlike his various contemporaries in the Triads, Lee had chosen to divorce himself from Chinatown to some extent, procuring land and a decaying mansion from a haole businessman whose taste in decorations ran toward antebellum Dixie. Sweeping renovations had transformed the place into a rich-man's playpen, with a hard eye on security. The house and grounds were under round-the-clock surveillance, and a chopper waited on the helipad out back, a last resort if all else failed.

It could have been a relatively simple hit, in spite of Lee's precautions, if the Executioner was simply looking for a body count. An air strike or a mortar would have done the trick in style, but killing Ho Yuan Lee was only half the battle. Along with those he meant to take out of the play, the warrior had to think of Lisa Yau.

And bring her out alive if possible.

If she was even there.

It had been preying on his mind that Lee had stashed her somewhere else. There had to be a thousand different rat holes on Oahu, and he didn't even want to think about the other islands, readily accessible by air or water.

As well, he refused to dwell upon the possibility that Lisa might be dead. His fault, perhaps, for pushing Lee too far. Another life on Bolan's hands.

He caught himself and wiped the mental slate. No time for such distractions on the battlefield, where life and death depended on his clarity of mind and his ability to make split second choices under fire. If Lisa was alive, then he'd find her, and if not, he was prepared to punish those responsible.

Whichever way it went, Lee's borrowed time was running out.

He parked a mile from the estate, the dark sedan as secure as it could be within a roadside stand of trees. He thought about engaging the explosives, then decided not to bother. If he didn't make it back, there seemed no point in leaving booby traps for the patrolman or the tow truck driver who was summoned with reports of an abandoned vehicle.

He wore the nightsuit, face and hands blackened with war paint. He buckled on his gear and carried out a final check on each magazine and weapon, the Desert Eagle on his hip, the Beretta with its silencer beneath his armpit. Spare clips for both were in pouches circling his waist, plus half a dozen frag grenades to balance the load. A Ka-bar fighting knife was sheathed on his shoulder harness, a selection of incendiaries and garrotes secured in the pockets of his skinsuit.

Seeking to maximize firepower, Bolan selected the M-16/M-203 combo as his lead weapon. A bandolier of extra magazines and two of 40 mm rounds were added to his burden, strapped across his chest. It would be worth the extra weight if he encountered half the armed resistance he expected from the Chu Lien Pang.

The hike took twenty minutes, Bolan moving like a jungle cat and pausing frequently to check for outside sentries, booby traps or sensors. He expected Lee to strengthen his security, but there was no way to predict what form the new precautions might assume. More soldiers, certainly, but would they all be penned inside the walled estate? He couldn't take the chance, and moving slowly through the darkness, Bolan also had a chance to think.

About the proper angle of attack, for openers. The folly of attempting to retrieve a prisoner—alive—without support troops at his back.

He could have called on Tommy Anders for impromptu reinforcements, but it chilled him to imagine what would happen with civilians thrashing in the undergrowth by night, attempting to approach with stealth yet warning every gunner of their presence from a mile away. It could have been a massacre, all right, but not the sort that Bolan had in mind.

Alone he at least had a chance, however slim it might turn out to be.

He reached the outer wall of the estate without encountering resistance. It was seven feet in height, a coil of razor wire on top. He didn't bother checking out the gate, aware that gunners would be concentrated there. Instead he circled back along the wall, up-slope, until he found a banyan tree that overlooked the grounds. He slung the M-16 across his back and scrambled up until he found a decent branch extending toward the wall, a foot or so above the razor wire.

From Bolan's perch, he could survey a portion of the grounds and glimpse the house, which was half hidden by a stand of Norfolk pine and eucalyptus. At the moment he was more concerned with sentries and security devices, checking out the grass that gently sloped away from him beyond the wall.

The insulators fixed on upright metal posts, spaced out along the wall at twelve-foot intervals, informed him that the razor wire had been electrified. A pair of insulated cutters was attached to Bolan's belt, but he dismissed the thought at once, afraid that any break in the prevailing circuit might set off alarms inside the house. He needed time inside to gain the best position possible, and he couldn't afford to have an army rolling down on top of him the moment that he hit the ground.

No sentries were visible, so far, and he supposed they'd patrol on some established schedule. It would help to know exactly where the nearest gunners were, but he might wait and watch all night without result.

It was a chance that he'd have to take.

One more precaution for the road. He drew a silver whistle from a pocket of his skinsuit, blowing sharply as he kept his eyes fixed on the grounds. No sound was audible to human ears, but any dog within a quarter of a mile should hear the call and offer some response. If Lee employed attack dogs—even those prevented from announcing their approach by surgical removal of their vocal chords—they should be gathered at the wall beneath his tree in moments.

Bolan gave them ample time and then some, blowing on the whistle every ten or fifteen seconds for a full three minutes. Bolan finally put the toy away, his concentration shifting to the actual mechanics of his entry.

It would be a twelve-foot drop, considering his altitude above the fence, the slope beyond, but there was more involved than simply letting go and landing on his feet. The branch he occupied was thick enough to bear his weight, but it didn't extend across the wall. He'd be forced to clear the stone and razor wire in a leap that spanned the wall and dropped him on the sloping ground inside.

No sweat, unless he landed wrong and something snapped inside. Or slipped on takeoff, tumbling down into the wire. But there simply was no other way inside.

His mind made up, the warrior wasted no more time debating his decision. Rising from his crouch, he took a long step backward toward the trunk, then pushed off in the direction of the wall.

Below him, darkness opened like a yawning throat.

IN NORMAL CIRCUMSTANCES stand-up comics seldom carry firearms, and they almost never creep around in darkness, looking for an opportunity to start a war. In that respect, at least, it would be safe to say that Tommy Anders was exceptional.

The mini-Uzi seemed to weigh a ton, though Anders knew that it was really more like twelve or thirteen pounds, with the suppressor and a fully loaded magazine. The extra clips were stashed inside the pockets of an Army-surplus jacket he'd picked up at a thrift shop hours earlier. The jacket might be hot, but it concealed a multitude of sins.

The target was a bathhouse on Auahi, patronized by Yakuza who liked to take their relaxation in the old-world style. Wong Yau had been for striking at the Triads first, but Anders managed to resolve the argument by cutting cards, a method that had never failed him when he had a chance to stack the deck. Yau drew a jack, against Tsuyoshi Ino's ace, and he had settled for a promise that their second strike would be directed at the Chu Lien Pang.

Assuming any of them lived that long.

From observing and reporting, it was a long step into Bolan's world of midnight raids and free-fire zones. If Anders had been playing by the book instead of improvising as he went along, he never would have found himself outside the bathhouse, waiting in the darkness with a dozen vigilantes waiting to repay old wounds in blood.

The bulk of them were younger men, and all were packing weapons of their own when they assembled in the parking lot outside Yau's office, ready to begin the hunt. Most were armed with handguns, several shotguns, with a rifle here and there. Anders took one Uzi for himself and let the others take what they could carry.

He'd marked the bathhouse as a long shot, figuring the Honolulu Yakuza would be standing guard around their master, or pursuing new assaults against the Chu Lien Pang. To his surprise they counted fifteen soldiers entering the spa within a short half hour, Ino and Toshiro naming each in turn, affirming their connections to the syndicate.

Ten minutes passed without a new arrival, so the hunters made their move. Tsuyoshi Ino led the way, with younger men on either side and Anders close behind, several others bringing up the rear. Outside, Toshiro kept four gunners for himself and sealed the exits, cutting off their enemies' escape.

A Japanese receptionist was smiling as they entered, losing it as guns came into view. She was directed toward the street and hit the sidewalk running, disappearing in the dark without a backward glance.

A sort of air lock stood between them and the baths, with swinging doors on either end. Beyond, a locker room and showers flanked the entryway, the steaming baths dead ahead.

On Anders's left a pair of tattooed men were standing naked under shower heads and gaping at the new arrivals. To the right another stood before an open locker, slacks in hand. The rest had made it to the baths, lounging in the water, soaking up its warmth.

He was expecting it, and still the gunfire startled Tommy Anders, ringing in his ears. A shotgun blast took out the soldier on his right, before the guy could drop his pants and reach the pistol he'd stashed inside his locker. In the shower stalls a waist-high burst from one of the Uzis dropped the other two and left them twitching on the tiles.

There was instant chaos in the bathhouse as they fell upon the other Yakuza, no quarter asked or granted. Several of the tattooed thugs had pistols tucked inside their folded towels, within arm's reach, and they were scrambling for the weapons when the raiders opened fire in unison from twenty feet away.

It lasted all of thirty seconds, bullets smacking into flesh and tile, some plunking into water that had taken on the color of a vintage claret. Illustrated bodies thrashed in the tubs or writhed on the floor, reminding Anders of a seething viper's nest. A couple of the naked gunners reached their weapons, but their hasty rounds were wasted, as determined shooters cut them down.

The sudden stillness was as shocking in its way as anything that went before. A glance at his companions told the comic they were all intact, though some of them looked stunned by the carnage they had wrought.

So much the better, Anders thought. It shouldn't be an easy thing, like reaching out to swat a fly. The killing might be necessary, but it shouldn't be a game.

"We're out of time," he snapped. "Let's move it."

Toshiro's backup team came running as they reached the cars, all sorry they'd missed the show. Next time, the comic thought, any one of them could have his ringside seat.

But he recognized the comment as a lie and kept it to himself. Next time—within the hour, if their luck held out—he'd be on the firing line once more. Against another enemy.

HER PRISON HAD NO WINDOWS, and a single door. The furnishings consisted of a folding cot and a plastic bucket, with a naked light bulb in a metal cage above. There was no switch inside her cell, but Lisa didn't mind the light. At least no secret terrors could approach her, as they might if it was dark.

She'd been handcuffed in the car, the bracelets leaving angry welts around her wrists, although the stunning blow to Lisa's head had rendered her incapable of serious resistance. Now she probed the tender spot behind her ear with gentle fingers, tracing the erratic outline of a scab where blood had matted in her hair.

No major damage, she decided, though it hurt like hell. Her vision had been fuzzy for a short time after she awoke, and fear of some unspecified internal injury had momentarily replaced the shock of her abduction. As she recovered from the blow, her headache dwindling to a focal point behind her eyes, the greater fear returned.

And with it, feelings of betrayal.

Sam Jiangsu had tricked her, set her up, although his motives were impossible to fathom. Somehow he'd been recruited by the enemy, convinced to turn against her father and support the Chu Lien Pang. It struck her, with a pang of wounded vanity, that her dislike of Sam had been misplaced. He didn't want her body, after all; he'd been laughing at her, laughing at them all, reporting every conversation to the Triads in return for... what?

Her "uncle" didn't live beyond his means, though she supposed there might be secret bank accounts, perhaps a safe-deposit box. He didn't spend the money on expensive cars or clothing, and despite her own suspicions of his lechery, the fact remained that she'd never seen him with a woman other than his secretary or his sister, while she was alive.

A mystery. As Lisa scanned her barren cell, she wondered whether she would live to see it solved.

The fleeting thought of death brought back another memory, of Andrew's face, the windshield of his car disintegrating with the impact of a shotgun blast. Imagination did the rest, supplying graphic details, and she reached the plastic bucket just in time, her stomach giving up its contents in a steaming rush.

The spasm passed, and Lisa stretched out on her cot. The pain behind her eyes was there to stay, but otherwise she felt a little better. It surprised her that she had no tears to spare, but crying would have been a waste of energy. She needed all her wits about her now if she was going to survive.

The Triads needed her for something, and it followed that she'd be used as bait, against her father. A demand of money seemed too commonplace, but there were other kinds of ransom. Lisa, under lock and key, provided leverage that might compel her father to betray Belasko, Tommy Anders and the rest.

Alive, she might unwittingly destroy them all.

The thought of suicide occurred to her, and she experienced a feeling of relief at finding no apparent weapons in the room. In any case her death wouldn't eliminate the risk to others if Ho Lee concealed the fact, and he could hardly be expected to announce it.

To spare her father and the rest, she must escape. But how?

She double-checked the room. There was no doorknob on her side, as if the chamber had been specifically designed for hostages. A ceiling vent—the air conditioner—

was out of reach and barely large enough for one of Lisa's arms, in any case.

That left a confrontation with her jailers, if and when they came for her again. She'd been undisturbed since her arrival, but her watch was gone, and Lisa had no concrete grasp of time. It stood to reason they would feed her sometime, or at least retrieve the bucket for a dumping. She just might stand a chance if one man came alone.

Seduce him? The idea made Lisa smile. It was a gambit from the kind of exploitation movies where the heavies are a pack of idiots, convinced that every woman in the world craves nothing more than rape. A movie jailer would be easily deceived by phony passion, lured to his doom without a second thought, but her abductors were professionals, without a moron in the crowd. Whatever Lisa hoped to get from them, she'd obtain by force alone.

And she'd need a weapon.

Glancing at the bucket, Lisa thought that she could fling its contents in his eyes, then strike him with the pail while he was blind. The plastic wouldn't crack a human skull, but if she put sufficient force behind it—maybe sticking out a leg to help—it might do well enough to knock him down. From there, if she could reach his gun . . .

What gun? And if there was a weapon, could she bring herself to use it? Yes. On that account she had no doubts at all.

An unarmed man would ruin everything. She wouldn't have the strength to strangle him bare-handed, and a plastic pail had its limitations as a killing tool. If he was bringing food there might be something useful on the tray. A knife and fork, perhaps.

The thought revolted her. She was prepared to shoot a man—Ho Lee, perhaps—if it would help her family, but hacking him to death with silverware was something else.

She had a plan, of sorts, and there was nothing more that she could do. Imagining diverse scenarios wouldn't prepare her for the fact of confrontation, and her plan would come to nothing if they sent two men.

Committed, Lisa drew the pail a little closer, concentrating on the door and blocking out the smell. She'd have little warning when they came. Her cell was nearly soundproof, and for all she knew, the house might have been deserted.

She could only wait and try to hold her fears at bay, preparing for the moment that might save her life.

Or end it.

19

The drop was more like fifteen feet, a slight miscalculation, but he tucked his legs the way they taught in jump school, M-16 against his chest, and made it with a shoulder roll that brought him to a combat crouch, his weapon leveled at the darkness.

Bolan half expected someone to start firing at him, but the shadows seemed indifferent to his presence. Moving out in the direction of the house, he stayed alert, convinced there'd be sentries covering the grounds. If he surprised one on patrol there'd be ways of coping with the problem, but if one of *them* took Bolan by surprise, the shit would hit the fan.

He picked up number one a moment later, still two hundred yards from target, standing with his back against a tree and smoking. It was bad enough that anyone with experience could track him by the smoke and glowing ember of his cigarette, but standing as he was, the lookout also left his flanks exposed.

He took the sentry with a textbook move, approaching from behind, the tree between them, circling to the right when he was close enough to touch the guy without a stretch. No warning, as he clamped one hand across the gunner's mouth and brought the Ka-bar up to draw a crimson smile across his throat from ear to ear. The dead man struggled for a moment, instincts letting go of life with grim reluctance, but the puppet dance was brief and futile. Bolan lowered him to earth with care, to keep from making any sound.

He wiped the blade, retrieved his M-16 and took the time to lift a compact walkie-talkie from the dead man's belt. Concealment of the corpse would be a waste of time if they were keeping tabs by radio. The sentry would be missed at change of shift, whenever that was, or a good deal sooner if the yard boss tried to raise him on the air. From that point, it would be a game of seek-and-fetch, but Bolan planned to have his own play in the works by then.

Resuming the approach, he covered half the distance to the house before he found the next two lookouts. Bolan couldn't tell if they were tapped to work in pairs, or one of them had simply left his post in search of company. They spoke Chinese, not even bothering to whisper, and he navigated on their voices for a dozen strides before he had the men in sight.

The shooter on his left was grinning as the other told a story, cradling a riot shotgun in his arms. His partner had an AK-47 with a folding stock, and Bolan knew at once that he could rule out slipping up behind them with a knife. No matter how he sliced it, one of them would have the time to fire a shot. It didn't have to score; the noise alone would be enough to queer his play.

But they'd have to go.

He knelt and laid the M-16 beside him on the grass before he palmed the silenced Beretta. Lining up the shot, he sighted first on the lookout with the shotgun, because his hand was closer to the trigger. Number two was more relaxed, the AK-47 dangling from a grip around the muzzle, and he'd require a crucial moment to reverse the hold.

At twenty feet he slammed a parabellum mangler through the left-hand sentry's grinning face. The impact took him down without a grunt of protest, thrashing for an instant on the grass before chaotic signals from his brain subsided into silence.

Number two used up the last split second of his life attempting to decipher what had happened to his friend. Before he had a chance to turn and face his executioner, the next slug found its mark behind his ear and dumped him on his face.

Two up, two down.

His question of a moment earlier was answered after Bolan checked the bodies and discovered only one of them was carrying a radio. It stood to reason, then, that lookouts closer to the house had been assigned to work in pairs. If they were all as careless . . .

Bolan shrugged the thought away. He couldn't count on anything tonight. If Ho Lee's gunners were relaxed it had to be from confidence in the security arrangements. They were used to having things their own way on Oahu, and the risks of all-out war were canceled, in their minds, by the protection found in numbers.

Bolan had already shaved the odds a trifle, but he still had far to go. One hundred yards, in fact, and when he cut the stretch by half, he was presented with a long view of the driveway, curving toward the house across a broad expanse of lawn. He'd have had a hard time picking out the distant gate, except for headlights that abruptly lanced the darkness, casting tiny figures of the posted guards in silhouette.

More lights behind the first, and Bolan froze, intent on learning whether these were reinforcements summoned from the streets, or someone else.

He got his answer as a burst of automatic fire erupted from the lead car, scattering the guards. They answered on the run, then he saw a fire team racing from the house, across the lawn, to back the pickets up.

No time for calculating who the new arrivals were or what they had in mind. The warrior saw his opening and sprinted for the house, intent on taking full advantage of the armed diversion while it lasted.

Close, now. Lisa would be in the house or else she wouldn't. Either way, the show of force told Bolan that his quarry was at home. If Lisa had been hidden somewhere else, Ho Lee would show him where. If all went well the Triad chief could be their ticket out.

SACHIRO MATSUMOTO had been disappointed when his boss announced that he'd lead the final raid against Ho Lee himself. The Yakuza lieutenant had no right to argue, and he kept his reservations to himself, beyond a cautious admonition that the leader of the clan was too important to be risked in battle. It did no good, and Matsumoto had resigned himself to riding in the second limousine as they approached Lee's gate.

With any luck he still might have a chance to bag the Triad chief before Taoka stole the show.

It would have been a small thing, fit for conversation over tea or sake, but Sachiro had been privy to the messages from Tokyo. He read between the lines, absorbed their tone and knew the leaders of Ichiwa-kai were having second thoughts about Taoka's leadership. The Honolulu boss had been insulted and humiliated by a gang of Chinese, and while the act of seeking counsel from superiors was technically correct, it left Taoka looking weak and indecisive. There were times, Sachiro knew, when it was better to proceed with strength and courage, acting on one's own initiative, than to delay and wait for orders from above.

His instincts told him Tokyo would welcome a replacement for Taoka once the present difficulty was resolved. Their choice would be a man of action, able to defend the family against all enemies, and any gesture Matsumoto made, betweentimes, would be filed away for future reference.

The single-handed execution of Ho Lee, for instance.

Never mind that Kenji had insisted on participating in the raid. Sachiro had been calling for decisive action since the crack of dawn, and he'd led the other strikes against their enemy himself. If he could find Ho Lee in the confusion of the raid and pick him off before Taoka had the chance, Sachiro's stock would be substantially increased.

Of course it would be better still if something happened to Taoka in the middle of the raid. A lucky bullet from the Chu Lien Pang, perhaps.

A lucky shot from *somewhere.*

They managed sixty-five on Round Top Drive, four cars in line, with thirty gunners plus Matsumoto and Taoka. Slowing for the gate, he watched as Kenji's driver brought the Lincoln's nose within a foot of black wrought iron, his high-beam headlights nearly blinding four men on the gate.

A rear door opened on the driver's side, demands were issued and refused. He saw the muzzle-flash of automatic weapons as Taoka's gunner brought the gate men under fire, one going down before the others scattered left and right for cover.

"Wait," Matsumoto told his driver, flicking off the safety of the Daewoo automatic rifle wedged between his knees. "We must not press the boss."

On cue the lead car flashed its backup lights, retreating several yards before the driver dropped it into gear again and rammed the gate. It took three running starts before the sliding gate was battered off its track, and Matsumoto heard a grating sound that set his teeth on edge as Kenji's limousine scraped past the twisted barrier.

"Be ready," he commanded those behind him. "Follow your instructions to the letter, for the family."

Their orders weren't subject to interpretation—storm Lee's house and slaughter anyone they saw, until the leader of the Chu Lien Pang society was found. In no case should Ho Lee be killed before he was presented to the boss . . . or his lieutenant.

Matsumoto had supplied the final touch himself without Taoka's knowledge. If his choice of words was questioned it would be a simple matter to pretend that he was following instructions, planning to deliver Lee to Taoka for his punishment. A point of protocol, perhaps.

In fact, Taoka was so intent on preparing for the strike that he paid no attention to Matsumoto's turn of phrase. A servant of the Yakuza for over twenty years, Taoka took the loyalty of subordinates for granted, never dreaming that his lieutenant might have dark ambitions of his own.

A louder scraping sounded this time, like giant fingernails against a chalkboard, as Matsumoto's Lincoln shuddered past the gate. A bullet struck the armor-plated door beside him, but the Yakuza lieutenant never flinched.

Behind him, firing through a hidden gun port, one of Matsumoto's soldiers cut the Chinese marksman down. Inside the Lincoln, with the windows closed, the burst of automatic fire was deafening.

Matsumoto didn't mind. His moment had arrived, and the staccato sound was music to his ears.

Ho Lee was tired of waiting for the man called Bolan to arrive. At first, as darkness fell, the wait had preyed upon his nerves. But now it only made him angry. Lee hadn't secured his post as leader of the local Chu Lien Pang by letting enemies intimidate him, forcing him to dance while they picked out the tune.

If Bolan meant to kill him he would have to fight an army first. And in the meantime, Ho Yuan Lee could think of no good reason for ignoring Lisa Yau. She'd provide some entertainment while he waited.

Lee picked up a bodyguard on his way downstairs. He didn't fear the girl, but she was likely to resist, and he couldn't be seen grappling with her like a common thug. When she was properly subdued, by force if necessary, then she would be his to do with as he liked.

It was apparent from the last reports of Sam Jiangsu that Bolan had recruited allies of his own in Chinatown. Wong Yau was certainly among them, and before Lee dealt with Yau in person, it would serve the merchant right to know that Lisa had been forced to pay for his mistake.

If she was apt enough, and learned her lessons well, Lee might decide to spare her life. It seemed unlikely, but experience had taught him not to rule out any possibility before he gave it serious consideration.

Pausing at the door to Lisa's cell, he waited while his bodyguard flipped through a ring of keys and found the right one, bending to the lock. The door was barely open when a putrid smell assailed Lee's nostrils, and he knew that Lisa had been ill. It was a typical response to being knocked unconscious.

The guard preceded him, addressing Lisa in Chinese, commanding her to rise. Ho Lee had been expecting trouble from the girl, but her response surprised him even so.

Without a hint of warning, Lisa Yau scooped up her pail and dashed its reeking contents in the guard's face. He gasped and raised one hand to wipe his eyes, the other groping blindly for his pistol as she followed through. The pail was only plastic, but it made a solid cracking sound against his skull, the impact knocking him off balance. When she kicked him in the groin, the man gasped and doubled over, clutching wounded genitals.

The girl was reaching for his gun.

Enough.

She was amusing in her way, but Lee couldn't permit her to obtain a weapon. Moving with the sudden energy of youth, he struck her hard across the face and sent her sprawling across the cot. Before she could recover, Ho Lee was on top of her, the second blow just hard enough to leave her groggy and disoriented.

Seizing Lisa's wrist, he dragged her to her feet and bent the captive arm behind her back. A little pressure brought her to her toes, and Lee decided he would keep her there. It made a good beginning for her training in obedience.

He left the guard where he lay, still mumbling curses through his pain. When Lee was finished with the girl, he'd dispose of the man, weeding out the careless and incompetent as any gardener would, to let his precious flowers reach their full potential. Any soldier who couldn't subdue an unarmed woman wasn't worth the bullet it would take to end his life.

She tried to lose him on the stairs, a fumbled backward kick that grazed Lee's thigh. But he was ready for her, and he tripped her, putting extra pressure on the arm to lift her up again before she was prepared to stand. Her cheeks were wet with tears before they reached his bedroom, and he found it stimulating. She was like a cornered tigress, but the cat had met her match.

Inside, he wasted no time on preliminaries. Spinning her around, he kept a tight grip on her twisted arm and drove a short, swift punch into her solar plexus. Gasping, out of breath, she sprawled across the king-size bed, incapable of offering resistance as he knelt beside her.

Ho Lee hooked his fingers in the neck of Lisa's blouse and ripped it down the front, the buttons flying. With it went her bra, exposing milky breasts. Lee felt himself responding, his reaction magnified by Lisa's helplessness. He was fumbling with her slacks, the zipper taunting him, when gunfire echoed from the grounds.

Forgetting Lisa in an instant, Lee pushed off the bed and moved to stand before the nearest window. Muzzle-flashes winked and sputtered at the gate, and he watched a heavy vehicle begin to batter through the tough wrought iron.

He thought of Bolan instantly, then shrugged the notion off as one car breached the gate, a second close behind. And then another, followed by a fourth. His men were fanning out to rake the vehicles with automatic gunfire, the occupants responding as their cars rolled toward the house, unstoppable.

If not Bolan then who?

Taoka. Moving in to take advantage of Chu Lien Pang's distress.

Lee spit a curse and bent to draw a pistol from his nightstand. It was loaded, cocked and locked, the safety on. He flicked it off and reached for Lisa, clamping steely fingers on her arm before he dragged her to her feet.

Now that Lee had time to think about it, he was glad to see the Japanese. He had a chance to cripple Kenji's army tonight, and only two things could have pleased him more—to learn that Kenji was among them, fool enough to lead the raid himself, and thereby place his life in Ho Lee's hands, and to see Mack Bolan's body stretched out on the grass beside his other enemies.

It was a night of miracles, and Lee was hopeful that his every wish might yet come true. Still smiling, he pushed Lisa Yau across the threshold and along the hallway toward the stairs.

HE DIDN'T BOTHER with the front door, knowing Lee's commandos would be concentrated there, prepared to meet the hostile motorcade. Instead the Executioner veered around behind the house to reach a spacious patio that faced the built-in swimming pool.

There was a door, perhaps the kitchen, but he didn't like the odds. It only took one sniper to create a lethal bottleneck, and if he didn't score a kill, the shooter stood a decent chance of pinning Bolan down until his reinforcements could arrive and do the job.

A few yards farther on he spied glass sliding doors, the draperies drawn tight. He swung up the M-203 launcher and fired a high-explosive round dead center through the glass, already crouching as it detonated, spraying crystal shards across the patio. He followed with a burst of 5.56 mm tumblers from the M-16 and charged in through the smoke, alert to any visible reaction from his enemies.

No action in what seemed to be a sitting room, and Bolan kept on moving, through another door that put him in the dining room. He had his pick of exits this time, one ahead and one immediately on his left. Before he could decide, the door directly opposite burst open to admit a wiry gunner, spraying bullets from a compact submachine gun.

The kitchen sentry, sure, but he was at a disadvantage now, compelled to leave his post. A 3-round burst ripped through his chest before the guy could pin his target down, and Bolan watched him stagger backward, dying, through the door again and out of sight.

His choice made, Bolan shouldered through the nearer exit, dodging to his right and flattening against the wall as bullets scored the plaster overhead.

Two guns, or three?

Before he got around to a head count, Bolan needed cover, and the nearest was a heavy sofa ten or fifteen feet away. He made the lunge with automatic weapons heating up the air around him, bruising ribs as he came down upon the heavy bandoliers.

The sofa served its purpose, but it wouldn't last for long against the concentrated fire of several weapons. There were bits of stuffing in the air already, bullets punching through space between the thicker cushions. He knew that he'd have to cancel out the threat or find another place to hide.

He thumbed another high-explosive round into the launcher and primed it, rolling to his side for greater leverage when he made his move. The doomsday numbers running in his head were louder than the hostile fire that pinned him down.

On three.

He hit the magic number, snarling as he made his move with thunder in his hands.

20

"Pull over here. We have to do the rest of it on foot."

The Chinese driver glanced at Tommy Anders, got his confirmation from Wong Yau and coasted to a stop along the verge of Round Top Drive. The other two cars followed his lead. A hundred yards behind them, Ho Yuan Lee's estate appeared to be the setting for a private fireworks show.

"Okay, let's gather around."

Their last stop had been Waikiki, Taoka's stronghold on Nahua, but the place had been deserted. The last thing Anders wanted was to step on Bolan's toes, but he could no more turn the troops around than he could stop the surf from crashing under Diamond Head. If they were bound to risk their lives no matter what, at least the big guy's proximity might help to even out the odds.

He hadn't counted on a firestorm, though. If Anders read the sound effects correctly Ho Lee's compound was engaged in what could only be considered all-out war. A glimpse in passing had revealed the twisted gate, a body sprawled behind it, and the comic thought he knew where Kenji's troops had gone. More party crashers, and the odds were getting longer all the time.

Or were they?

"Anybody want to reconsider?" Anders asked, his answer coming in the form of stoic glares. "Okay, then.

Good news, bad news. You already saw the gate. I think Taoka's men are hitting Lee right now, and Mike Belasko should be in there, too. The good news is, the Yakuza and Triads may be killing one another off right now. The flip side makes it twice as many guns against the few we have. I'll ask again—''

"We haven't come this far to turn away," Wong Yau informed him sternly.

"All our enemies together," Tsuyoshi Ino said. "It's better than we hoped."

"We've had a run of luck so far," the comic told them. "Once we cross that line and mix it with the regulars, there's no way back. You have to know that going in."

"We're wasting time," Yau said.

"Okay, let's hit it. Do your best to stay together, and for God's sake, don't shoot any haoles dressed in black."

The smell of cordite met them at the gate, an offering of incense to the god of battle. Anders led the way inside, around the crumpled gate, past leaking corpses, the others on his heels.

And stepped into the middle of a free-fire zone.

He thought there should be something he could say to Yau and Ino, all the rest, but they were busy running, picking targets, finding cover on the field of battle.

"Screw it," Anders said. "Who wants to live forever, anyway?"

THE HIGH-EXPLOSIVE ROUND went off behind his enemies, the ruined door frame adding jagged chunks of wood and bits of mortar to the flying shrapnel. Bolan saw one gunner leveled by the blast, a portion of his skull sheared off, and all three guns went silent for a moment in the aftermath of the explosion.

Bolan used the fleeting time to his advantage, ready with the M-16 as he emerged from cover, closing on the enemy. He caught one gunner struggling to his feet and stitched him with a rising burst from crotch to throat, the dead man sprawling backward in a heap.

His partner had been wounded by a piece of shrapnel, but the SMG was in his hands and tracking Bolan as the Executioner released another burst of automatic fire. The tumblers caught his opposition with a finger on the trigger, and the Chinese shooter's dying burst etched out an abstract pattern on the ceiling.

Portrait of the artist as a corpse.

He fed the M-16 a fresh clip and left the dead in peace.

Beyond the smoking doorway, stairs offered access to an indoor balcony of sorts. He was expecting opposition, and the gunners didn't disappoint him, spraying anxious rounds and trying for a cross fire prematurely, when a glimpse was all they had.

Retreating, Bolan marked the shooters in his mind. Two on his right, crouched down inside the vestibule, with two more—maybe three—up on the balcony to his left. It was a decent set, and he'd have to take them all before he could proceed.

He chose a 40 mm buckshot round to feed the launcher, then unclipped a frag grenade and weighed it in his palm. It narrowed down to timing, with a chance to sweep the field if Bolan played his hand correctly. If he faltered, any one of four or five young guns could drop him in his tracks, and that would also mean the end of Lisa Yau.

Assuming she was still alive, and Ho Lee hadn't panicked at the sound of gunfire. If the Triad leader chose to cut his losses . . .

Bolan shrugged the morbid thoughts away and braced himself in preparation for his move. The frag grenade was in his left hand, with the safety pin removed, the M-16/M-203 suspended from his shoulder by its sling. A basic one-two punch, if he could pull it off.

He pitched the hand grenade on instinct, needing distance more than accuracy, since the vestibule was close to fifteen feet across. The gunners saw it coming, firing wildly after his retreating form, but there was nothing they could do to save themselves. One bolted, while the other hit a fetal curl and tried to ride it out. Both were cut to ribbons by the blast.

The upstairs gunners—three, he saw now—were shaken by the blast, and only one saw Bolan make his move. The guy was shouting something in Chinese, his automatic rifle tracking onto target acquisition, when the 40 mm launcher belched a storm of buckshot pellets toward the balcony.

The charge swept two of Bolan's enemies away and left the sole survivor wounded, clinging to the rail with one hand while he gripped a submachine gun with the other. Bolan stroked the trigger of his M-16 and finished it, a 5-round burst sufficient to retire the side.

No time to hesitate. Would Lisa be upstairs or down?

He chose the stairs, had nearly reached them when a faint sound reached his ears above the din of battle.

Had it been a woman's voice?

The warrior hesitated, listening, and heard the sound repeated. Yes. He couldn't swear that it was Lisa, but the voice was definitely feminine. Downstairs, beyond a corridor that lay to Bolan's right.

In the direction of the helipad.

Too late, his mind insisted, but the body couldn't let it go. He raced along the hallway, following the voice that might belong to Ho Lee's cook, a maid—or Lisa Yau.

The gunner heard him coming, waited for the perfect moment, counting Bolan's steps before he sprang the trap. The linen closet made a perfect hiding place if you were small and didn't mind the waiting game.

Caught up in the pursuit of Lisa Yau and Ho Yuan Lee, the Executioner was taken absolutely by surprise. One moment he was sprinting down the corridor, pursuing distant sounds. The next, a closet door slammed open, almost in his face, and Bolan met his enemy at point-blank range, the automatic pistol rising in his hands and squeezing off two rounds.

Directly into Bolan's chest.

SACHIRO MATSUMOTO crouched behind the Lincoln, listening as bullets drummed like hailstones on the armored body. If he craned his neck he had a fair shot at the house, but Ho Lee's gunmen had been laying down a heavy cover fire, preventing anyone from getting close enough to slip inside.

It was a stalemate, and to Matsumoto, a draw on hostile ground was a defeat. Lee's house was fairly isolated, but they'd been making noise enough to wake the dead these past few minutes, and he knew that someone, somewhere, would inevitably call the police. Worse yet, the stalemate gave Ho Lee a chance to summon reinforcements from the city, and Sachiro's people might be trapped inside the grounds at any moment, their retreat cut off by hostile guns.

The time had come to salvage what they could and slip away before they were annihilated on the spot. The limousines would function—three of them, at least; the point car had a steam cloud rising from its crumpled hood—and with the losses they'd suffered, Matsumoto reckoned three would be enough.

Defeat would be humiliating, granted, but they'd inflicted losses on the enemy, and they could finish it another day.

He risked a glance across the Lincoln's hood and saw Taoka, huddled against the first car on his left. Matsumoto knew he wouldn't have another opportunity like this again.

He waddled toward the back end of the Lincoln, staying under cover, with the Daewoo automatic rifle helping him maintain his balance. From the darkness on his left, a Triad gunner suddenly appeared, unsteady on his feet, blood streaming down his face from ragged scalp wounds. He was dazed, disoriented, but Matsumoto saw the pistol in his hand and stitched a burst across his chest before the gunman had a chance to recognize his mortal enemy.

No quarter asked, none given.

It was time for Taoka now. Matsumoto edged around the Lincoln until he found the proper angle, kneeling as he braced his forward elbow on the trunk. He framed the back of his boss's head within his sights and gently stroked the Daewoo's trigger, three rounds gone before he lifted off. Taoka's head exploded, spattering the limousine and those around him as he fell.

Before the startled Yakuza could comprehend their loss, Matsumoto was beside his fallen leader, cradling Taoka's shattered skull and shouting at the others, "Quickly, to the cars! We're outnumbered here!"

He grudgingly delivered Kenji's body into other hands and scuttled toward his waiting limousine, the night alive with bullets cracking overhead. If they could only make it to the highway, put this place behind them. There was no one to contest his leadership of Honolulu's Yakuza.

His hand was on the door latch when a new barrage of fire erupted from behind the limousines, his driver pitching forward with a breathless grunt. A bullet grazed the Yakuza lieutenant's hip, another ripping through his shoulder, spinning him around and slamming him against the car.

It was impossible to focus through the pain and drifting smoke, but Matsumoto could have sworn his new assailants were Chinese and Japanese together. In other circumstances the absurdity of that idea would certainly have made him laugh, but at the moment he was in no mood to take a joke. His life was running out, and he didn't have strength enough to lift the rifle that had fallen in his lap.

Incredibly the gunman who stepped up to finish him was white. A haole round-eye in the midst of chaos, surfacing from nowhere as a pair of ancient enemies were locked in combat to the death. The submachine gun that he leveled at Matsumoto's chest was fitted with a silencer.

Beyond incredible, the dying mobster thought he recognized the gunman's face.

"I know you."

"Makes us even," the haole replied.

"You'll finish it?"

"I will."

He did.

DISTRACTED AS HE WAS, Ho Lee came close to letting Lisa Yau escape as they were coming down the stairs. She seemed to lose her footing, sagging back against him, and he eased the pressure on her arm a trifle when she gasped in pain. It was enough, and Lisa twisted in his grasp, a spitting cat, her free hand flashing toward his eyes with fingers hooked like talons.

Lee was quick enough to save his sight, although her fingernails dug bloody furrows in his cheek. He clipped her with the automatic pistol, and she wasn't faking this time when her legs went slack. Instead of loosening his grip again, however, Lee increased the pressure, forcing Lisa up on tiptoes and propelling her downstairs.

His enemies were in the house. There was no other explanation for the gunfire and explosions, close enough to bring the plaster raining down upon his head. How many? Lee had no idea, nor did he care. The time had come for flight, and his escape had been prepared.

No one could stop him now.

It was a shame about the girl. He wouldn't have a chance to know her body, but there were always other women, other times. Survival was the first priority, and Lisa Yau could help him there. The Yakuza might hesitate to shoot a woman, and if not, at least she'd provide him with a shield.

Her body would in fact be serving Lee, regardless of the interruption in their bedroom games.

He met a guard in the hallway leading to the helipad, a younger man whose name escaped him at the moment. Still, the man knew Lee and recognized his duty. He made no complaint when Lee instructed him to hide inside the linen closet and ensure that they weren't disturbed before they reached the waiting helicopter.

Life insurance.

They were nearly at the exit when his captive tried to break away once more. Lee gave her credit for determination, but he didn't have the time to toy with fools. When Lisa tried to kick him he swept her feet from under her and let her fall. Once she was down, he did the kicking, landing heavy blows against her ribs and thighs.

She cursed him, wailing, but the pain short-circuited resistance. When he tangled fingers in her hair and dragged her upright, leveling the pistol at her face, she wept but didn't struggle.

As gunfire rattled in the hall behind them Lee didn't look back. If there was danger on his heels he didn't wish to see it coming. They had time enough to reach the chopper. Time enough to fly.

The pilot had been waiting with his aircraft since the first alert of strangers at the gate. Lee didn't have to ask if he was ready; there were standing orders for response to an emergency, and failure on the pilot's part would be rewarded with a slow and painful death. Lee cherished loyalty in the few subordinates who might be called upon to save his life, enforcing their respect and childlike fealty through combinations of reward and punishment. A soldier who was faithful could expect the best of everything, from clothes and cash to women of his choice. The punishment for slackers ranged from fines and beatings to the screaming agony of death and torture, based upon the gravity of the offense.

It was an ancient system, tested over centuries in China, and it seldom failed. The pilot would be waiting for them with his engine running.

Ho Lee was nearly dragging Lisa by the time they reached the helipad, infuriated by her lagging. Did he really need the woman now that safety was within his grasp? What value would she have in days to come, as reinforcements were received for Ho Lee's war against the Yakuza?

The answer was apparent. She was useless to him now, and she'd have to die.

Relieved that the decision had been made, he gave a jerk on Lisa's arm that dropped her to her knees. He merely had to aim the pistol.

When the helicopter blew, the shock wave lifted Ho Lee off his feet and hurled him to the pavement, the impact driving all the breath out of his lungs. Bits and pieces of the aircraft fell to earth, some burning, and he caught the sick-sweet smell of gasoline before the spilling fuel erupted into flame.

He'd be burning, too, unless he dragged himself away.

Exerting desperate strength Lee didn't know he had, the leader of the Chu Lien Pang society first struggled to his hands and knees, then lurched erect.

To stare death in the face.

THE KEVLAR VEST SAVED Bolan's life, but it couldn't repeal the laws of physics, and the force of point-blank gunshots slammed him off his feet. There was an instant when he thought his heart had stopped, the throbbing pain between his ribs was so intense, but he couldn't afford the luxury of passing out or waiting for the hurt to go away.

Above him, grinning like a ghoul and leveling his pistol for another shot—perhaps the head, this time—his adversary seemed to be a giant, terrible and strong. In Bolan's world you dealt with hostile giants by the only means available.

You kicked them in the balls, or shot them, as the case might be.

Not close enough to kick this time, Bolan used the M-16, one-handed, holding down the trigger as he emptied out the magazine and let the muzzle climb. Twenty-five hot rounds remained inside the clip, and Bolan let the gunner have them all between the knees and chin. The guy performed a jerky little dance in celebration of his death, clothes rippling with the impact, spouting crimson here and there in jets that spattered on the rug, the walls.

Ringing silence reigned as the broken puppet fell away.

The pain got worse as Bolan scrambled to his feet, reloading first the M-16, then the M-203 with a high-explosive round. He knew Ho Lee was making for the helicopter—might be there already—and he was prepared to bring the aircraft down by one means or another. Anything was better than allowing him to flee, with Lisa or without her, to begin the game anew.

A few long strides, and Bolan had regained some measure of his balance, drawing shallow breaths to ease the throbbing in his chest. He felt light-headed, like a winded distance runner, as he reached the door and tumbled through, the night breeze soft and warm against his face.

Thirty feet away, Ho Lee was on the helipad with Lisa kneeling at his feet. He had a pistol leveled at her face, the helicopter warming up behind him, rotors gaining speed.

Instinctively he fired the M-203 launcher from his hip, the HE round exploding in the helicopter's cockpit. The concussion dropped Ho Lee facedown against the tarmac, but he held the pistol fast.

And struggled slowly, tortuously to his feet.

The hill chief's eyes came into focus, and he stared at Bolan, working out the riddle in his mind and putting it together.

"You."

"It's over," Bolan told him.

Ho Lee shook his head, still punchy, but refusing to believe.

"You can't stop the Chu Lien Pang."

"I'm stopping you," the Executioner replied. "For now that's plenty."

Lee's face went deadpan, but his eyes were burning, staring Bolan down. He telegraphed the move before it came, his battered body lurching as he raised the pistol, squeezing off two rapid rounds before he had a target in his sights.

The M-16 beat out a short tattoo, and Ho Lee shuddered, twisting as the 5.56 mm bullets ripped across his rib cage, blowing him away. He got off one more shot before he hit the tarmac, fired in the direction of the moon.

Long strides put Bolan at the side of Lisa Yau. He pulled her blouse together in the front and was about to help her up when scuffling footsteps on the pavement brought him back around to face the house, his automatic rifle leveled at the face of Tommy Anders.

"Whoa," the comic said. "I've had some bad reviews, but this is getting out of hand."

The warrior let himself relax, identifying several of the men at Anders's back.

"We done here?" Anders asked.

Wong Yau came out of nowhere, running, dignity forgotten as he gathered Lisa in his arms. Far away, in the direction of the city, Bolan heard a siren's mournful wail.

"We're done," he said. "For now."

Bolan is no stranger to the hellfire trail.

DON PENDLETON's

MACK BOLAN.®

HARDLINE

Corrupt electronics tycoons are out to make a killing by selling
ultrasecret military hardware to anyone with the cash. One of
their targets is a man with one foot in the grave, an occult-
obsessed defense contractor.

Mack Bolan finds himself enmeshed in a mission that grows
more bizarre by the minute, involving spirits and Stealth,
mystics and murderers.

Available in December at your favorite retail outlet, or order your copy now by sending your
name, address, zip or postal code, along with a check or money order for $4.99, plus 75¢
postage and handling ($1.00 in Canada), payable to Gold Eagle Books to:

In the U.S.	In Canada
Gold Eagle Books	Gold Eagle Books
3010 Walden Ave.	P.O. Box 609
P.O. Box 1325	Fort Erie, Ontario
Buffalo, NY 14269-1325	L2A 5X3

Please specify book title with your order.
Canadian residents add applicable federal and provincial taxes.

SB25R

AGENTS

IN THE DEA, SUDDEN DEATH IS THE PRICE OF FAILURE.

SHAKEDOWN

PAUL MALONE

DEA agent Jack Fowler follows a thin white line to Jamaica's tourist paradise to crack down on a heavy new cocaine network. Posing as a dealer, he puts his life on the line, taking on a ruthless, violent enemy and a legal system that often conspires against justice. Alone in a jungle of cops on the take, he's doing a slow burn in the deadly heat of enemy fire.

Catch the fire of Gold Eagle action in SHAKEDOWN by Paul Malone, the third book in the AGENTS miniseries.